Ezulwini
Place of heaven

Jayne Galassi

First published 2006 by David Philip Publishers, an imprint of
New Africa Books (Pty) Ltd, 99 Garfield Road, Claremont 7700, South Africa

www.newafricabooks.co.za

© text: Jayne Galassi, 2006
© published work: New Africa Books

This book is copyright under the Berne Convention. In terms of the Copyright Act, No. 98 of 1978, no part of this book may be reproduced or transmitted in any form or by any means, electronic or mechanical, including photocopying, recording or by any information storage and retrieval system, without permission in writing from the Publisher.

10 digit ISBN: 0-86486-681-X
13 digit ISBN: 978-0-86486-681-3

Editing: Rosamund Haden
Layout and design: McKore Graphics
Cover: Petaldesign
Proofreading: Tessa Kennedy

Printed and bound in the Republic of South Africa by Shumani Printers

AUTHOR'S NOTE

This is a novel set in a time and place that is as authentic as I remember it. I have allowed the main character, Gillian, to borrow selectively from my own childhood, but that is where the resemblance ends. If you recognize other characters in this book, it may be because they exemplify individuals we have all met in the recent history of this continent. This might have been the history of any white child growing up in Africa at the time.

As for the leopard, she is as real and true as the legend of her kind.

> This book is dedicated to my mother, as sure and
> true as the mountains,
> and my sister Annie for her love and wisdom.

I know that the Lord has given you this land and that your terror has fallen upon us, so that all who live in this country are afraid because of you.

Joshua 2: 8-9.

I have often looked for myself... I have gazed at this face in the mirror... but I could never say I have seen myself. For when I seek myself, it is exactly the same... that is both seeker and sought.

Marcilio Ficino

PART ONE

The beginning

Thomas told me that he had only really believed in God once. It was when we lived with Gaga and PapaMac in Swaziland, at the time of the leopard, he said. If that were true, then God existed for just a little over two years — for my brother anyway.

He didn't speak about it again, but that leopard was at the heart of the consequences that changed all of our lives fifty years ago. She is the reason I have come back.

Shaba — Thomas had given her the name — was the watcher on the hill, the immortal Osiris. Our secret. She walked in the garden at night, past the hydrangeas, the agapanthus and the roses that shone white in the moonlight and over the damp kikuyu grass where the scent of lavender settled fresh and sweet in the dew. She knew the boundaries of the thatched white house, and the paths that led from it, past the small round room at the back and up to the servants' compound, behind the pungent lantana bushes and the red-hot pokers where the chicken sheds were kept. More than once she pilfered a live chicken that scratched in the dirt outside the wire coop and nestled in a shallow ditch near the lime-washed walls.

She would have been familiar with the sound of voices and music, the smoke of the coal fire and the smell of the old dog that never strayed far from the door. Perhaps she had a sense, too, of a boy and a girl who rolled on the terraced lawns and traced their fingers through the dirt, rubbed their palms against the bark of trees and left the smell of bare feet on the sand.

The Swazi people call her Ingwe, the African leopard, mother spirit and soul of the ancient Pard. She has been called thief or murderer in fierce antipathy and fear. For centuries she has taken from the abundance of the land, adapting when necessary to change and hardship, because she has learnt to be cunning and persistent, overcoming adversity and surviving in spite of it. She is both beautiful and terrifying.

Her domain has been steadily eroded and encroached upon but she is still queen on mountain slopes and the rugged hills between small towns. It has been to her advantage that she is a silent and solitary hunter, slipping in and out of the moon shadows, finding her prey wherever it is offered, waiting and watching from high places, for opportunity, for chance. She knows the way the land lies, the hiding places, the smell of the soil. Generations of her kind have learnt the habits of rodents, wild pig, zebra and antelope. She has even learnt the ways of men, of shepherd boys that are careless, and rusted latches on chicken sheds and broken fences on goat pens. She is familiar with open burial grounds in dark forests where dead children lie with the wasted corpses of old men outside villages that thrum to the sound of drumming like a still beating heart. She shadows the fear of dreaming men.

The night Thomas stopped believing, as on most other nights, while the children lay listening to the sounds that only darkness brings, the leopard ran quiet as a secret, down the stone path through the wooden gateposts that gave off the sharp odour of bitumen, and between the rows of lettuces and spinach where a vegetable garden grew neatly in the damp soil and the air held the fragrance of mint and parsley. Passing the boundaries of the garden she would have followed a footpath that led through a thicket of poplars and wild wattles, and upwards towards the top of the hill. Beyond that, the mountain rose through the mists, the back of a sleeping monolith turned against the night sky and the moon. From a granite ledge on the mountain she would have had a wide view of the farmlands and the gum tree forests, the white house on the hill and the green valley they called Ezulwini, the Place of Heaven.

II

From Ermelo the road deteriorates, pitted and pot-holed and truck weary. The bus lurches past unsuspecting bakkies towards the highlands. As we near the Oshoek border, grey granite mountains ascend from deep valleys gold with grass, and rounded boulders announce the start of Swazi terrain.

Through the window and my own reflection there, I touch the gentle billowing of valley and hill and the flat bedrock sprouting grass tufts like soft tails. My fingers know the feel of curling lichen like splashed paint on rough rock.

Once slow and lazy, cradled in the heart of a wilderness shadowed by the Dlangeni Mountains, Mbabane now shines in Western drag, neon, glass and glare, a plastic valley – Surf: Bright like New, Bright like You. Banners and billboards are bright with pleas. Virginity is a good word, teach it to your children. Trust Condoms. Men can make a difference.

The town has evolved into something foreign and I am on the periphery, a traveller, seeing it with new eyes. Coming back has transformed the past into fiction. What I remember is a story that seems to hang by itself in a timeless space like so many other stories that must have begun here, a few caught and collected like anecdotes, but most lost.

I have arrived at Mbabane, weighed down with tinned and dehydrated fruit and vegetables, books and art materials, a suitcase of less than appropriate clothing, and my greying hair already shrinking and rising into a coir tangle with the damp.

I am lost in the longing for something old (in stone walls, cracked concrete sidewalks, old faces in old windows), still looking for ghosts from behind my sunglasses, when Winston's bearded face appears in front of me. He grabs my elbow like a handle and steers my delinquent-looking luggage and me towards his Land Rover.

Winston feels no obligation to engage in small talk; you could hardly converse anyway over the rattle and clatter of the Rover grinding along the narrow, pitted road to Siteke. He and his wife are old hands, so familiar with this game that they have assumed that tough and weathered camouflage that hides the colour of their humanness in this khaki bosveld. They are one of those rare couples, a National Geographic relationship, no children, no fixed abode, they live solely for their work in the field of diverse and daring exploits. It's a transient existence I have often envied from the distant shores of motherhood and suburban banality. So, I shall be dithering about in the background of Winston and Maggie Brandt's more professional pursuits: the serious game of capturing the untamed for the curiosity of city people. I am here as an observer of the nature of the beast.

'We have found her lair,' Winston says. 'There are two cubs.'

'How long have you been tracking her?'

'This is our fourth week. She's been unusually co-operative.'

'I can't wait to see her.'

'Tonight. We're hoping to film her again tonight.'

I watch tawny veld grass blur past the window, flat lowveld bristling with umbrella trees and thorny sickle bush – mud and stick houses where poverty and the virus live side by side like discarded bedfellows.

Winston swings the jeep up the winding hill into Siteke for petrol and supplies. A corrugated shack no larger than a long-drop boasts a hand-written slogan – Use my Phone for 80c. Winston has disappeared into the Don't Worry Grocery. I wait in the jeep, my mind whirling in non-recognition of what I once knew as Stegi.

Memory stirs as we drive slowly past the Stegi Hotel, and I am sitting on the clean lawn of a whitewashed hotel in the sun-drenched afternoon listening to the tinkle of bone china teacups, silver spoons, gramophone music and frivolity. If I close my eyes I might still hear the hollow thwack of tennis balls, see Mum out there on the veranda sipping gin with the white-clad golfers who laugh about straying impalas or the odd kudu wandering onto the greens. Stegi was always a slow town.

With my eyes open, I see only the present. The once rolling lawns languish under weeds and litter, and shrubs that were trimmed and neat have grown tired, tangled, tardy. I turn my face away, swallowing the store of tears that sometimes attend regret. On the steps of Siteki's once fashionable Bamboo Inn, a sombre group of traditional healers gather in the evening chill. Who will save the children now?

From here Winston will drive us northwards, into the sublime wilderness of the Lubombos. On the other side of this plateau are the coastal areas of Mozambique and northern KwaZulu-Natal. From Siteki, if you look back, the straight road disappears over the plains, into the blue hills and mountains of the highlands, and you can measure the entire width of one of the smallest kingdoms in the world.

III

I have begun to explore that time, and this place, turning over the stones with careful deliberation as we had often done on the hill, anticipating the scorpions hidden underneath.

It is not surprising that I remember the dining room so vividly. It is here in the centre of the house that the family meets for the evening meal, the conclusion of the day, the last sentence on a page before bed.

The long table is highly polished mahogany. It is laid in a formal arrangement of English porcelain and silverware. Here between the props, restraint and polite conversation are scripted in a code, the Queen's good manners. An electric candelabrum hangs above the table, which is arranged with PapaMac's homegrown greens, Gaga's toils from the groaning Arga stove, and, when his mood is generous, the Dad's sanguinary and gruesome concoctions.

The table is a stage and dinner time is a nightly performance, with each act announced by the ringing of a small brass bell. The bell is placed in the centre of the table. The children are forbidden to touch it – but we do.

The bell is a bonneted Victorian lady with a skirt that is delicately engraved with floral filigree. The ringing is sharp and surprisingly loud. The skirted lady is polished to a warm golden sheen and stands centre stage on a white cotton cloth, broderie anglaise, surrounded by dainty porcelain dishes, gravy boats and silver spoons. My grandmother lifts her and tinkles ceremoniously two or three times with an abrupt flick of the wrist, then muffles the sound on a folded serviette.

The sound is enough to summon the kitchen girl, who enters the swinging door almost immediately, barefoot in clean starched white cotton. She enters quietly, eyes cast down, and will curtsy whether serving or taking away the dishes. She never speaks at all in the dining room. Except for the fact that she is black, she is like a starched white ghost that appears and disappears conveniently, in and out with the ringing of the small brass bell.

Our lives are made comfortable with servers. Servants. Invisible people who take care of the mess, in the kitchens and laundries, the gardens and outhouses. Natives with biblical names, because the names they are given are not easy on the English tongue.

Our grandmother was a large lady rarely seen without a hat. That's how other people remember her. She had lived most of her life in the company of ladies who needed to be seen as accessories to their husbands' prosperity. They had strutted through the fashionable streets of Rosebank in Johannesburg with shopping bags of distinction, like multi-layered birds pecking through the miscellany of imported bric-a-brac from Europe and the Empire.

Although GagaMac's sense of style was born mostly of an unsophisticated eclecticism, it was she who insisted on oriental carpets of the finest silk, art nouveau statues and vases from London and original paintings and prints from the fashionable galleries in Johannesburg. Her lounge was furnished with floral couches and chairs covered in Sanderson linen with embroidered antimacassars on the arms and headrests, tall reading lamps with tassled silk shades that spilt warm circles of light on French-polished ball-and-claw side tables, each dressed with a cotton doily and an Italian glass ashtray. The window drapes were of heavy velvet, a deep plum colour, with gold brocade on the pelmets.

When PapaMac was forced into early retirement because of his heart condition Gaga found herself limited to the periphery of diminutive Mbabane with its one main street, two rows of functional shops and a post office. Here was a safe haven, PapaMac said, with all the beauty and wilderness of Africa without the native trouble that was brewing in the townships to the south.

My grandmother shut herself away in the big house, choosing to turn her back on the smothering gossip of 'small town people who lived and breathed in each other's pockets'. She had stored away most of her exotic finery in a stinkwood kist with heavy brass finishes that stood at the end of the grand wooden beds in her bedroom. These were her private treasures, memories of a different time, and she would visit them some afternoons like old friends, touching them with fond regret for the life they embodied, not only in the cities of the colony but in the England of her childhood.

Despite her outward display of finery, my grandmother was not like other society ladies: her dreams and premonitions had set her apart. PapaMac did not disguise his contempt for her implausible presentiments, even when the wind blew into our lives a strange sequence of coincidences that might have absolved her of this disdain. He called it 'Harriet's foolishness'. PapaMac was sensible and a man of moderation. Like his one dram of good Scots whisky and one cigarette after dinner, his prescribed limits were never exceeded and he had little tolerance for those who did.

Gaga managed to keep her strange insights well hidden most of the time, but now and again there was a slip of Foolishness that caught PapaMac by surprise and provoked his exasperation. My grandmother seemed to have organized the running of her house with the same restraint, as if an ordered perfection would keep the visions away and in denying herself she would reap the rewards of acceptance. If the mirrors were sullied and reflected a less than clear image of mortal substance, she might fall apart.

Her grandchildren were thus a constant threat to her compulsive routines and we often suffered the backlash of her frustration. Thomas, because he was boisterous and moved through the house like a whirlwind, sending antimacassars flying, knocking over kitchen chairs, traipsing mud through the passages, and me because I was a day-dreamer and forgot things – like leaving the bath water running till it flooded the carpets, spilling milk because I forgot to hold my cup straight, leaving crumbs on polished floors. There was an endless list. We were always ducking a clip on the ear, a slap on the legs, running from her explosive anger that rang through the house and made your ears burn with shame.

For her part, my mother could not be bothered with the extravagancies of GagaMac's world. She was the first working woman in the family. PapaMac had agreed, reluctantly at first, to send her to a university although he did not think higher education necessary or useful for girls. But he was pleased with the results and credited himself with her practical application of learning, her logical mind, her dedication to educating others. An educated woman was a credit to a deserving husband.

By the time I arrived my brother Thomas had already been here for three years and was openly unenthusiastic about sharing his mother. He learnt reluctantly to tolerate the competition. In the scheme of things my birth was a mistake ill-timed in a marriage that was teetering on the brink of disintegration. The place of my untimely arrival was Johannesburg, South Africa.

Unremarkably, I remember nothing much at all before the age of five. So that is where this story begins, at least for me, and by then we had left Jo'burg and had settled here in the small British Protectorate of Swaziland, east of the former Transvaal.

Even after that, however, there are only snatches of remembering. The record of this journey in time is true at its core, in the way it was felt, but I may have filled some of the spaces with what never happened. The recollecting and the telling of history have proved unreliable since the beginning of time; in our very humanness we are forgetters. So, at the end of it all there are only windows of wakefulness where the senses are sharp or emotions piqued in bliss or sheer terror. The rest, the crumbs that are left, are merely fabrications like family snapshots, on small themes of little consequence.

IV

This is my first memory.

It is in my fifth year and the ants have come to carry away our house. PapaMac drove his Pontiac all the way from Jo'burg to bring us to Swaziland. Just the three of us. We left our Dad behind.

My mother has found a teaching post at the local school and an affordable cottage, a rondavel with one room, a bathroom, and a kitchenette on the side. Thomas and I have pet white mice that smell of Jungle Oats in a temporary cage in the garage. A huge snake comes in one morning uninvited, and eats the mice. He lies there like a lumpy stuffed stocking on the floor after his lunch. We scream in terror of the snake and sob at the loss of the mice. Looking back I can see that he did not mean to expose himself and his gargantuan appetite to the innocence of children. Unlike one I came to know, who did it deliberately and hoped that I would see.

That morning of my fifth year I look up and see that the thatch is curiously red and moving in ripples like water. My brother pulls the sleeve of our sleeping Mum.

Hey, the roof's falling on the bed in bits.

But then the bits start biting like they don't want people to be there.

Mum screams — Ants! And we grab some stuff and run outside. We stand there watching, as if the place is burning to the ground. But it's far worse, our Mum says, We could have been eaten alive.

We never go back to the rondavel. We leave it to the ants.

Our new home is smaller, but at least there are two bedrooms, and a corrugated tin khaya at the back with a 'live-in' Swazi maid called Esther who comes with the lease. Mum finds this useful, as she'll be teaching every morning, and I am not yet 'ready for school'.

Neither is Esther, as it turns out, even though she seems grown up, so the two of us have something in common from the start. Mum gives careful instructions about diet, cleanliness and supervision. Esther and I nod while Mum's words float in pretty colours over our heads and out the door. I loved the sound of her voice.

Do you understand, Esther?

Yes'm. Good'm — she has a huge white smile and twenty odd words of English, and Mum believes her. She loses trust in Esther in about six weeks and is forced to make alternative arrangements, but before then I have gained a considerable education.

There is a bramble forest behind the house, a maze of wild berry-laden bramble bushes with stay-a-while thorns, and black wattles and poplar trees. It is here that I lose my sense of direction, never to find it again. But Esther always finds me, a blonde head amongst the berries. We traipse hand in hand back to her khaya and sit on paraffin cans where we dunk chunks of buttered white bread in tin cups of sweet milky tea and eat stiff salted porridge with buttered fingers.

The khaya is dark and damp and the walls smell of acrid soot and candle wax. Esther smells of Lifebuoy carbolic and an ointment for a million uses called Zambuck. She brushes her beautiful white teeth with salt, and sniffs tobacco powder from a tin so it makes her sneeze like pepper does. I have never yet met anyone who took such pleasure from a sneeze.

'Where's your bath?' I ask her. She laughs. I hold my hands against her belly when she laughs. It wobbles like a jelly.

Her bath is a zinc basin the size of a birdbath, but she manages to wash in it, one piece at a time, and puts herself together again all clean and smelling of Lifebuoy. I squat on my haunches and watch avidly. I come to know the ritual well, pointing out the next stage, like a manager of body washing.

I try once to reach out and cup the weight of Esther's pendulous bosom in the palm of my hand and Esther gurgles and pushes me away, her breasts swaying like ripe fruit. Nakedness in Esther's dark khaya is a mysterious and secret pleasure, folds of brown flesh like soft shoe leather; it smells of earth and coal tar.

More naked than her ebony body is Esther's uncovered head. She removes her scarf like a bandana bandage to reveal a tight carpet of coir curls. I am amazed and privileged to be an audience to this spectacle because it is something Esther shares only with me. She sometimes walks out of the khaya with her breasts swinging bare under the washing line, but she never removes her headdress outside the darkness of her khaya.

In spite of the few words between us, we begin to depend on one another. I lead her into the secrets of our house, exploring the curious collection of bottles in the bathroom cupboard and the treasure of old lipsticks, trinkets and loose change in Mum's dressing table drawers. Esther introduces me to her world, a rusted biscuit tin that stores little jars of Vicks and Vaseline and remnants of old soap bars, a broken porcelain duck that she uses as a candleholder, and a cardboard box of various white madams' cast-off junk, a collection of useless mementoes that keep me occupied for hours.

When it becomes clear that I have begun to show a preference for primitive rituals, like eating with my hands, discarding my shoes and blouses and addressing my conversations in broken Swazi, our Mum becomes alarmed. She arrives home one day to find me half-naked, coming out of the bramble forest stained purple with evidence of a feast. Her voice is high with alarm like a bird, then buzzes like a thousand angry bees. The bees swarm round Esther's head until she clutches it and wails. She cries rivers of tears that spill a wet patch on her apron-covered bosom.

The khaya door is shut and locked and Esther is sent away forever.

V

After that, there came Veronica. I can't really put a face to the name of Veronica, other than the face I last saw her with, which wasn't really hers.

There is an Auntie standing over my mother who is sitting on a chair in the kitchen.

They think I am invisible. That is because I am sitting on the floor, sharing a box of uncooked macaroni with my friend Noj. Only I can see him, to the others he is invisible. His real name is Jon, but it suits him better backwards. I am translating the conversation into whispers and sign language for him because he cannot understand anyone but me.

My Mum says: I never really liked her from the start. One of those modern girls, you know.

A blurrie-cheeky-black — think the world owes them, says the Auntie.

My mother adds, She had shifty eyes, know what I mean? Still, if Papa hadn't insisted, I never would have called the police in.

She swiped them from under your nose! the Auntie snorts.

She took them out of my bedside drawer. I actually saw her wearing them on her day off!

The Auntie makes a clicking noise with her tongue. But they all do it, hey? Like they're entitled to help themselves!

Oh well, I don't know. She was — cheeky — you know. But the police... what they're like. If there had been any other way...

Agh, Pammie, she'll get what she deserves, make no mistake... Are those the ones? Aren't they pretty?

With my grown-up mind I see the scene as clearly as if it were playing out before me.

I stand and run to the table, resting my chin on my hands to see better the earrings that lie side by side there. Two little green stones. I lift Noj up to see.

A van draws up outside. Doors slam and there are men's voices. I hear a small dog whining in the street. Mum and the Auntie peer through the window.

Mum sucks in air and shoves her fist against her mouth.

Ja, well that's that then. It's O.K. She'll get over it. She's learnt her lesson. Best tell her to clear out her things and leave in the morning. That's what the Auntie says.

Oh God, my mother keeps repeating. Oh God. Oh God.

I squeeze between them, dragging Noj behind me.

'We want to see the puppy!' I say.

Mum grips my arm to pull me away.

But I see her anyway. There's no puppy after all. It is Veronica with a bloody face, plum red on her black skin. Her eyes are swollen shut and she is whimpering like a puppy, stumbling across the lawn.

When I think of Veronica, that's the face I remember.

VI

I am forced to accompany my mother and Thomas to school every morning, even though it is still agreed that I am not yet ready for it. All attempts at enrolling me at a nursery school have failed, as I find the raw and primitive tribe of four and five year olds terrifying.

I spend the last few months of my too-young-for-school year at the back of my mother's remedial classroom. I am in my wax crayon stage, drawing the habitual curly-headed trees with lollipop trunks. I draw in wax while my mother attempts to educate the lost boys from never-never land. The boys are all ages, shapes and sizes, and some are clearly less school-ready than me. Her voice drifts over their heads in soft colours on a patient tone of blue. In the comfort of her voice, I feel that safe enfolding sense of Mother and I wish I could sit here forever, drawing and smelling wax in the back of the remedial classroom.

A boy whose ruddy knees have outgrown his short pants by far comes in late after break one morning, holding his head and blabbering like a baby. He has streaks of dirt running down his face like camouflage stripes, from his crew-cut hair to his chin.

'He t'rew me wif a stone, Miss.'

My mother's compassionate nature is overruled by her immediate sense of English language propriety. As young as I am, I know that the boy has stepped onto dangerous ground with that aberration of language. Afrikaans translated directly into English is an unforgivable misdemeanour for Mother the teacher. It takes priority over any playground bashing.

'Did he pick you up and throw you together with the stone?' she asks stiffly.

The boy says, 'Huh?'

'We don't say, threw me with a stone. Do we, Class?'

'No, Miss!'

'We say: He threw a stone at me. Don't we Class?'

The boy with the striped face sits down, sliding his knobbly knees under his desk.

'Maar hy't my met 'n klip gegooi,' he insists. In his own language it is real and hurts in spite of the grammar, as does the bruising shame of being different.

But my mother is not unkind. She takes his hand and leads him up to the sickbay where he is washed clean and bandaged.

I think it was then that I realized it was only me who felt that unconditional safety in the sense of Mother. To them she was only

Miss and to her they were the lost boys. She knew that some would make it and some wouldn't, and she was right about that.

My mother was right about most things when I was that young, but there were things I was beginning to discover on my own. I was beginning to understand the difference between preconceived perception and real observation, my first stepping stone into a soul-coded career as an artist.

I am six years old now and in the first grade, drawing a wax crayon garden with wax crayon trees on a curved horizon, above which hangs a yellow-fingered sun. I think it is the sheer boredom of watching several carbon copies of the same tedious old format that brings our teacher, Mrs Dawson, to despair. She ushers us out single file onto a playing field soldiered by real trees reaching up to the blue Swazi sky.

'You need to see a tree to draw it,' she says. 'Look up there, at the branches. How they reach up and grow smaller branches, and then smaller still, until each twig grows little leaves. Little leaves in bunches. See the sky peeping through? Like hundreds of little blue windows?'

I have never really seen a tree before. Six years old and I only have pictures in my mind of what the world appears to be. Now I know that you have to understand the shape of things to be able to see. I translate this newly found knowledge into discovering the shape of my world. My destiny is wrapped in the kernel of that precise moment when I learn to see a tree.

VII

Discerning even the most obvious discrepancies in one's own parents was less definable.

I had a misplaced concept of my father as a generous man. When

I spoke of him to friends at school I said, My father is a kind and generous man. For years he sat upon that pedestal, like a favoured museum bronze in the cloisters of my misinformed imaginings. This was a result of our last encounter with him, a tearoom, a strawberry milkshake and an iced doughnut.

It was just the three of us: my brother Thomas and I in a tearoom with our Dad. He's come all the way from Johannesburg to say goodbye. This is nothing new, he has said goodbye so many times before, it has become a family ritual. I know his face well. He has smiling eyes with friendly creases around them, and a broad smile not unlike my own, but I hardly know the man behind the face. We have lived most of my short lifetime without him.

He gives us each a menu.

'Order anything you want.'

'Anything?' Thomas says.

'Sure, anything.'

It's just a Coca-Cola tearoom with plastic tablecloths and neon lights on the main street of Mbabane. There are penny sweets in big glass bottles on the counter. Nigger balls and sherbet, rock candy, butterscotch and strawberry suckers, pink heart sweets with messages that read 'sweetheart' and 'love me do' and shoe laces made of liquorice.

'I'll have a shilling for sweets,' I say.

He ruffles my hair.

'Afterwards,' he says. 'How about a milkshake and some cake?'

I nod and grin at my brother, who sits stiffly in his chair, not saying a word.

'Milkshakes all round?' says our generous Dad with the laughing eyes.

We both nod mutely.

He tries asking some boring questions about school, and What do you kids do for fun round here?

But we don't answer. I watch for a cue from my brother who usually talks all the time, but he just stares into his glass full of chocolate bubbles.

There is a time when you're young that you seem to live only in the moment you're in, as if it takes all your reserves just to grow and learn the names of things. That must be why I don't remember being pulled over the neighbour's wall in the night or hiding in the linen cupboard with Thomas till it was safe to come out. If I had heard my father's voice rising on the cadence of drunken dispute and Mum crying in the night like a gramophone record, I must have forgotten. Perhaps I thought that's how things were meant to be. Like the colour of a tearoom wall that matches my strawberry milkshake the day our Dad came to say goodbye.

I only saw him again twenty-two years later, a sad old man with the prematurely lined face of someone whose life had been too quickly spent on cigarettes and brandy.

VIII

The limited resources of her independence eventually defeated our mother. She had done her best to maintain her self-sufficiency as a single divorced parent, and had borne the shame of this status humbly and alone. In those days the stigma attached to divorce was a social rejection that went far beyond the boundaries of church dogma and into the lounges and dining rooms of 'nice' society. Women bore the brunt of blame when a marriage could not be held together if only for the children's sake, dear. My mother wore Guilt on her stooping shoulders like a wet cardigan. She passively accepted the knocks that came her way as though they were her due. Even her remarkable intelligence was demurely worn under the tablecloth of good housekeeping.

When the demands her two children made on her time and her scant teacher's salary became too much, we moved into Gaga and PapaMac's house. I was almost six and Thomas was nine. It was November 1957.

Gaga and PapaMac's house was surrounded by mountains and hills where gumtree forests spilt into the gorges and valleys. It stood alone, nestled on Melagwane hill, an autonomous island imported from the Empire and surrounded by the wild and unpredictable flavours of an African landscape. It was a gracious old homestead wearing a wide thatched roof not unlike one of Gaga's summer straw hats, topped by two stone chimneys. PapaMac had called it 'Little Ezulwini' (Place of Heaven) after the green valley not far from the capital, Mbabane.

The house, enfolded by a spacious garden and an abundance of trees, was a never-ending playground for Thomas and me. It was fenced only on one side, all the way down the side of the only dirt road for miles, the nameless dirt road that wound its way down Melagwane hill.

From the back of the house a wide terraced lawn swept down to a sapling pinewood PapaMac had planted and on the lower side of the pines there was a flat outcrop of granite rocks, interspersed with wild grasses, aloes and thorn bushes. On the left of the house were natural rockeries where hibiscus and poinsettia shrubs grew as tall as trees, with azaleas, heavy with magenta brackets, and an abundance of thick sword ferns in between.

From there you would walk a stone path past the main house towards the kitchen and the separate rondavel or down a deeply shaded path to Papa's vegetable garden. Beyond the rows of carefully cultivated greens, and through the gap in the box-trimmed privet hedge, you stepped into the stark sun-bleached open veld, rugged and rock-strewn, that stretched up towards the top of the hill.

Gaga's front garden was a wide, sloping lawn surrounded by a gravelled circular driveway. The lawn stopped abruptly at the foot of a natural rockery where blue-headed lizards lived, and laced about the house and lawns were garden beds, abundant in seasonal flowers, my grandmother's pleasures.

The hill behind the house, 'our hill', was not grand enough to be called a mountain, though there were sheer granite rock faces and steep embankments on the other side. From the top one could see the whole of the valley and on the eastern side the Mdimba Mountains, which were pitted with caves that had once given shelter to the Swazis retreating from marauding Zulus. As I was to learn later, some of those caves were the sacred burial places of former kings, the dark cloisters of a Ryder Haggard underworld.

From the back of the hill rose the Dlangeni Mountains where leopards roamed and families of baboons took shelter, steenbokke, rock hyrax and other smaller creatures slipped in and out of sharp shadows. The Black Umbuluzi River and the Usutu meandered through the valley and wound their way across the Lubombos to Mozambique and eventually to the Indian Ocean.

IX

We have only been here at Gaga and Papa's house for a few weeks and I have decided to run away. I can't begin to remember the reason why, but perhaps it is because my grandmother is a fiery old dragon and no amount of sulking will soften her as it might have done my mother.

So I am leaving with Noj, a hand-me-down cardboard suitcase, an apple and a second pair of shoes. No particular reason for the shoes, except they are shiny new red patent-leather ones and will walk with me in my new life when I find it.

As it happens, that begins and ends at the front gate. The house is barely visible from the gate. Dust-green willow wattles bow wearily over the whitewashed gateposts. The rough dirt road rises up steeply from the right, and disappears around an uncertain bend to the left. I am not sure where either way ends or begins and am beginning to sense some reluctance on the part of Noj, but I stand firm in my resolve to embrace this adventure and cross the dirt road.

Distant sounds of rhythmic chanting assail my ears almost immediately – as if I had crossed a threshold and my defiance had been shouted from the hills to the whole world. For minutes on end I stand in frozen immobility while a chanting beast heaves itself up the hill towards me. The animal reveals itself in a steady roar of voice, deep and resonant, that holds a high calling note followed by a series of deep hollow whoops. I run back to the sanctuary of the gate and climb into the branches of a mimosa, watching breathlessly.

The coming of the beasts, for now it is clear they are many, is declared in a rising cloud of dust. My mind has foreseen a stampede of buffaloes following the winding road to the gate and turning into the drive, crushing Gaga's hydrangeas and dragon flowers and uprooting the jacarandas before smashing down the door, traipsing mud all over the Chinese silk carpet in the lounge.

Thrilled and terrified, I have grown into wattle branches with leaf fingers and yellow mimosa hair.

Then I see the colourful feathers bobbing up and down on the curve of the road, like the tails of dancing birds. Above the plumes, knobbed sticks rise and fall with the sound that now comes in waves. Then heads appear, the hair on some teased and feathered, some bleached yellow like mielie-cob tufts. Swaying and stamping the ground as they sing, warriors are marching to a war but with spears and knobkerries – no guns. Wattle gum, mimosa pollen and dust assail my nostrils. Too afraid to sneeze, I watch in terror the mass of semi-naked men stamp past to the rhythm of their song.

Then, in the sea of dark faces appears one man I know; so familiar yet shining, transformed. Used to his dress of soil-stained blue overalls I am surprised by Solomon the Warrior in a headdress of fine feathers, around his waist a leopard skin skirt and a bright red and white cloth tied diagonally across his chest. He raises the dappled cowhide shield high above his head, a spear blade flashes like a mirror to the sun. Commonly disguised as my Gaga's garden boy, he has hidden this other side from us. Here he is proud, perhaps a little dangerous. Our own Solomon is a soldier and the secret is mine.

Relaxing my fierce grip on the wattle branch as the last of the men follow the throng down and round the bend in the road, I stiffly sit up on my perch, dizzy with the danger of secrets and the possibility of detection. One of the stragglers at the back suddenly turns on his heel and, with a determined sense of direction, lifts his eyes to my hiding place and gazes at me as if he has known all along, as if they'd all known the deceit of my hidden watching. This one carries no shield or spear, but a whip like a severed horse's tail. His hair is mud-caked in red earth and knotted with ringlets and beads. He turns back, flicks his hair whip over his shoulder and disappears with the others out of sight.

Slowly the dust settles and grasshoppers and beetles resume their busyness in the hum of the summer heat

I remember all this vividly as I write.

As I returned down the winding drive towards the house it struck me how many of them there were. There were over three hundred men marching down the road that day, soldiers of the amaSwazi. It was only later that I found that out.

X

'What you saw is the calling of the people for Incwala.' I am sitting on the back lawn, hugging my knees and watching Martha, her thick brown arms elbow deep in soapsuds in a large zinc tub on the grass.

Martha is not a true Swazi, as I was to learn. Her Swazi mother had grown up on the outskirts of Big Bend near the border of Zululand in the north, on the other side of the great mountain. Martha had been educated at an Anglican mission school on the Natal side of Pongola, and later in Eshowe. Here she had learnt to read and write in English and attended the mission church where she came to know and love the white man's God.

Martha was a 'kholwa', a Christian native, as her mother had been, and as such she considered herself above the rituals of her own kind even though there were certain beliefs she could not let go of. There were many like her in Zululand, led by the church towards the rewards of heaven. Martha's father, a traditional chief as was his father before him, had embraced some of the Christian traditions and gained favour with the government, but his clan still adhered to the old customs.

When she returned to the kraal of her father's people, Martha found she could no longer accept in her heart the old laws based on a tradition of ancestral spirits, witch doctors and polygamy. Nevertheless, she obeyed her father's wishes and married a respected Zulu man according to custom. She bore him three children who were given Zulu names, but were baptized at the mission and registered in

Eshowe with their biblical names first. The day her husband took his fourth wife, a girl not much older than her youngest daughter, was the day Martha left the green hills of Zululand and her husband's kraal forever. She was not permitted to take her children with her. Their grandmother would mother them.

Martha sent her family a postal order from Mbabane every month and wrote letters, even though she never received a reply. In her mature years she had returned to the place of her mother's people and the well-worn pages of the Good Book that had sustained her faith in the face of a life she'd patiently endured but never fully embraced.

Now Martha is my nanny, witness to the family's most private secrets, allowed free access to bathrooms, cupboards and bedrooms, the dreams and whispers of other people's children. My Martha is enfolded into the life of our home by day, slipping into her own invisible life until morning. I know the warmth of her hands, the smell of her skin. Charge and servant, we are bound together.

'This is not war that they make at Incwala,' she says, and I watch her wet red-brown knuckles as she rubs the foaming clothes vigorously on the face of the zinc scrubbing board. I scoop up a handful of bubbles and watch the sun kiss them with a million rainbows before they pop and shrink on my fingers.

'Every year this must come. Incwala time. They call it the time of the first fruits. Say this please.' Her voice is smooth as dark brown honey. Martha is my teacher.

'The time of the first fruits,' I repeat.

'Good.'

'But why was Solomon there?'

'Why? Because he is Swazi too. He must run with the men.'

'But why is he dressed like that?'

'The king says so.'

The kings of my storybooks are cloaked in velvet and wear stockings and bejewelled crowns of gold. Our Queen Elizabeth, the real one, is so far away over the sea in England that I am sure that she wouldn't notice how we dressed in Africa – not that I am allowed much freedom in the matter of dress.

Our Mum has a harsh word for children who go out in grubby clothes, especially girls. She calls them poorwhites. I know it is something to be ashamed of, especially when it could apply to me. I hate squeezing my feet into shoes and socks to go to town, bows in my hair and stiff petticoats, double-layered and scratchy.

At home, however, here at Gaga's house, I can run and climb barefoot and feel the damp grass beneath my feet. As long as there are no visitors, Mum doesn't seem to mind us being poorwhites in the garden. Perhaps the king doesn't mind Solomon being a poorwhite and dressing in dirty blue overalls as long as he is in the garden too.

When I stamp into the kitchen, whooping the warriors' call, Gaga is angry.

'I'll have none of that savagery in here,' she says, her back to me, while she sorts ironed and starched white serviettes and folds clean linen into a drawer. I try to slip past her into the passage, but she swings round and glares, taking in the grubby knees, the bare feet, that unkempt look that shames my mother. She tut-tuts irritably and, with a sweep of her hand, gestures towards the kitchen girl hovering in the corner.

'Take the umfaan and wash lo face and lo hands with manzi and lo sepe.' As she speaks she indicates everything in sign language, not sure how much this new girl understands.

'All right, Precious?'

Precious, or 'Prayshus' as Martha calls her, nods and curtsies and hurries me out the door to the bathroom. I am not sure how much she understands either, so I reserve my conversation and she speaks in short breathless Swazi sentences while she lathers a facecloth and wipes the traces of my adventure from my face and hands.

Martha is still training 'Prayshus' in the ways of the household. Vegetable preparation and table setting are her tasks. All the effort and toil goes into the evening meal, which Gaga undertakes herself once the vegetables are scrubbed and peeled and the Arga stove is fired up and made ready. Lunch is never much more than bread and home-made jam and tea.

Every day, Solomon brings in a bucket of coal and cleans and feeds the hungry furnace. The coalhouse is at the back and an open passageway runs the length of the double garage to the back door so that the coal can be wheeled in a barrow and emptied into buckets for the fire. The coal truck delivers once a month. There are two manholes on the flat roof of the coalhouse and Solomon climbs the ladder and empties the hessian bags of their black contents into its dark belly. In the winter a brass bucket of shining black coal stands on the hearth in the lounge and a fire is lit every night.

The coalhouse is my most favourite place in the world. It is my ship and the back lawn my sea. Afternoons find me in the bowels of my ship surrounded by oceans of my making. It is Solomon who usually coaxes me out and lifts me in his arms and into the safekeeping of Martha, who quickly washes away all evidence of the child captain's voyage and saves her from Gaga's lashing tongue.

Most of my days are taken up in the pursuit of wild and capricious adventures of pretend, where Noj appears and disappears as my co-conspirator until one day I can no longer find him.

Martha is never far away. It is she who dresses me, bathes me, and sees to the first two meals of the day although I am almost six and perfectly able. Nevertheless, early independence and the ineptitudes that go with it are not encouraged.

After dinner Thomas and I rival for our mother's attention. Pestering her for stories and dragging out our nightly prayers, we find every excuse to prolong our precious time with her. She is listless and exhausted by evening and burdened with worry and she sighs between sentences.

My mother's voice has begun to lose its colour.

XI

For my brother and me, Little Ezulwini with its garden filled with dark hideaways, tall trees and wide lawns that never end, really is a place of heaven; we are cradled in a sanctuary of untroubled bliss never to be found again.

But even Paradise has serpents. There are creatures that hide in the shadows, living things that dart away, slithering into dark cool places beyond one's reach, and leaving the imagination in turmoil.

Snakes, often imagined but rarely seen, are a lurking possibility felt behind you in the hair at the nape of the neck, in quick fingers darting for a lost ball in the shrubberies, between the rocks in the garden, sudden death amongst the lilies and ferns that grow along the damp shady edges of the path to the vegetable garden: green mambas, spitting cobras, night adders and puff adders, and a green boomslang that almost landed on Thomas's head one day when it dropped out of the jacaranda tree at his feet and slithered past him up the lawn towards the road.

More often than not the fear of creeping things seeds unfounded imaginings, and rustling lizards and lazy earthworms are the victims of needless slaughter by reason of mistaken identity.

Apart from snakes there are scorpions that crawl under the doors and lie waiting in the folds of clothes or towels on the bedroom floors, making it imperative, beyond good manners, not to leave one's things lying around. There are other dangers too. Don't eat berries from shrubs or green hedges. Oleanders are poisonous, so are elephant ears. PapaMac tours the garden with us, never without his grey hat and silk waistcoat, to point out the poisonous plants. Just a lick of that and you'll be dead, he mumbles matter-of-factly. The danger posed by the berries, it seems, is that they harbour the eggs of black widow spiders.

In the summer, storms roll up the valley whipping giant sheets of lightning and startling the valleys and mountains with a cold and eerie light, followed by cracks of thunder so fierce Gaga says they wake the dead. Before the onset of rain, against a moody cloud-filled sky, the hadedahs fly above the house in flocks and cry an echoing ha-ha-haah! We know something you don't know. When those summer storms move over the basin of the valley you can see the lightning for miles across a bruised sky. We count the seconds between the thunder and lightning as it gathers momentum and rolls towards our hill.

It's the siren in the midst of it all that is the source of our real terror the first time we hear it, a mournful wailing that rises and falls in waves through the house and down the lawn and along the tops of the trees, and echoes in the valley like an Indian singing bowl. I cannot grow accustomed to the sound and am rooted to the floor in the horror of it, but Thomas is thrilled and fascinated. To him the sound announces battle cries and world war bombardment, imminent earthquakes or tidal waves. More than once he's turned on the switch of the siren during the day and risked a beating from our grandmother.

Ours is a second-hand siren with megaphone speakers that PapaMac seconded from an abandoned factory in Johannesburg and wired up himself to be triggered by electricity failure, common on the rural outskirts of the town. At the sound of the alarm Solomon runs down in the dark from the compound and Papa meets him with the torch. They make their way to the end of the garden and fumble about, often in the rain, for the switch in the electricity box. We keep candles in every room for just such an emergency; they flicker leaping shadows that lick up the walls and cause the house to mutate into a supernatural illusion of strangeness.

The alarm unnerves my mother. At the onset of a thunderstorm coming up from the valley in the middle of the night my mother will sometimes rise up from her bed, frantic and wild-haired, and run down the passage sliding her fingers along the wall to find the switch of the siren to stop the insanity before it begins.

I learnt later that our alarm was also a precaution against the possibility of marauding natives, just in case they turned their unrestrained barbarity upon their white protectors. It was whispered that trouble was brewing and the cold feet of the Motherland were poised for flight if the natives become too troublesome.

XII

When Thomas is sent off to board at St Marks in Mbabane, I quite suddenly become an only child. He comes home at weekends and holidays to punctuate his life with home cooking and barefoot abandon and has little time for a sibling three years his junior.

Thomas is my mentor and I follow him around like a wagging tail. If ever there was a good reason for my wanting to be a boy, it was envy of my brother. Compared with Thomas's world, mine is locked in a time warp. He brings us a taste of the real outside, of Elvis Presley and the jive, comic books and cream sodas, and the very latest in boarding school slang – Jeeslaik! Lekker! Helluva! Blurrie-hell!

Skop-skiet, Donder en Bliksum! Sprinkling Afrikaans in the Queen's English is forbidden, as frowned upon as blasphemy, Wicks bubble gum and nose-picking. Thomas groans at boarding-school food; he says Spirogyra for melon and ginger, Frogseggs for tapioca, Caesar's ghost for white blancmange, Snot an' noses for fried dumplings and custard. Agh sis, man! Everyone calls everyone man.

It's my job to Keep Cavey for Thomas and his friends, with strict instructions to call 'chips!' when someone is coming. Sworn to secrecy, cross-my-heart-and-hope-to-die, I sit with the 'big boys' and watch them smoking cigarettes at the bottom of the garden. I am chosen to steal Peter Stuyvesants from my mother's bedroom drawer. Who would suspect the youngest?

Thomas is an avid bioscope fanatic. He commits snatches of movie scripts to memory and performs them with exaggerated gusto to an audience of one, coming forth from behind the bedroom curtains and wearing his new character in changed voice and gesture. In spite of the dark curly hair and grey-blue eyes that belong to Thomas, I am easily transported by his changed persona into the different characters he becomes.

Home for the holidays, my brother goes into Mbabane every Saturday and Wednesday morning to spend sixpence on the bioscope at Queensway, a bottle of Coca-Cola, and to buy and swap comics. He has a pile of glossy American comic books in his cupboard that grows and shrinks with the swapping. In rare moments of magnanimity he allows me to read them, and he ticks them off on his list like a librarian.

Our Dad sends over Beano and Rover annuals from England for a while, until the distance between him and us dulls his paternal sentiments. Then it's the odd birthday and then nothing at all. He has sent me a large illustrated book called 'Pea Soup'. There are men in black suits and trilbies going off to work with their umbrellas, wandering through the streets of London in a blind thick fog. The book is so well scrutinized, the pages turned so often that eventually it falls apart, but I still can't find my father's tired face amongst the cartoon businessmen in trilby hats. Somewhere on the other side of the world my father is walking about in the yellow mists of a London Pea-soup Fog.

In rare moments, between shooting down German bombers and Messerschmitts, Thomas stoops through the door of my world. Near the house and surrounded by azaleas and poinsettias, on a dark bed of granite, is a column of stones almost as tall as I am, and Thomas and I dance around it like Indians round a totem pole. It is a mystical place we have baptized with exaggerated significance. There is a small brass plaque cemented in the top half that reads: Here lies Rufus, a trusted friend.

We hoped Rufus was a dead child, his brief life snuffed out in the Macs' garden, fallen from the top of one of the massive boulders in the rockery, or taken in broad daylight on the hill by a leopard or a hyena that mistook him for a baboon. Or it could have been a cobra bite, or a boomslang that paralysed him with a slow and terrible suffocation. But Rufus was a dog, we learn with some disappointment, a small black and white terrier who'd simply died of old age.

Still, Thomas finds my world of make-believe tiresome. His world is real, and he's at the centre, surrounded by friends. He is the voice, initiator of action and attitude, and a kid sister is an inconvenience hardly worth brothering with. Confident and strong-willed, he attracts social interaction as a matter of course; he is everything that I am not.

Thomas had not as yet begun to think about the leopard. That came later, after the time we got our new Dad. It is Thomas who first tells me we're getting a new Dad.

XIII

New dads are not on the list for Christmas, the catalogue from Jo'burg or the list for Mohammed's General Store. I'm not sure that Dads are particularly useful. Even if they are, you need to try them out first just to be sure it is the right one, like the dresses Mum tries on at Gresham's Dress Shop and sends back when they don't fit properly.

'We're getting him, voets-toets, like it or not. And if they think we're going to call him Dad, they're blurrie wrong!' He kicks at some loose stones as we come out of the poplar trees into the clearing above the green bowl valley.

We sit down on the rock ledge on the edge of a steep precipice that sweeps down to the wide road that the men on huge yellow graders are busy gouging into the mountain. Thomas leans back on his elbows, pulls on a shaft of sweet grass and chews it (dogs and jackals pee on grass, but he doesn't care). He runs his fingers through his unruly brown curls like a comb, like Elvis.

'So, how do you get a new Dad?' I ask.

'Mum's getting married, Dimwit.'

'Why?'

'Just because.'

'Who's gonna marry her?'

'Crikey Moses, it's bad enough having to call him Uncle Bryan when he's not even a relation!'

If my opinion is worth anything, I do not think it's a good idea either. My mother is marrying the man who eats silkworms.

In a child's mind, most of the past is soon forgotten in the sense of now, except the indelible instant that stirs the senses and leaves a streak of memory like a stain. Silkworm Time is one of those memories.

I have brought home a white Bata shoe box with compass-punched holes in the lid. I have been careful to fill the worm house with fresh mulberry leaves from the school-yard every other day. Last year I'd forgotten and found them weeks later under my bed, dried stick-worms that had shrivelled amongst the brittle leaves of a neglected landscape. My first attempt at motherhood was a miserable failure.

Silkworms aren't like other small creatures that fly into your hair and crawl uninvited into your space. They are slow and fatly gentle, nibbling their way to adulthood only to create one perfect masterpiece, a remarkable work of art that will carry each one through pubescence to a brief time of moth-motherhood. It is in the cocoon, the prized sarcophagus of worms woven in a gold silk thread, that the miracle happens, where these plump cold creatures somehow transform into grey feathered moths that come into a fleeting life for only one purpose, the laying of hundreds of eggs to start the cycle all over again. I have eleven whites and two zebras and by the size of them, my wormy friends are almost ready to spin.

I am sitting on the front steps with my nose in the shoe box when a strange man arrives in a dark green jeep, khaki-clad like a bush soldier. He wears sunglasses on his face and has a bristling moustache.

'Hello,' he says, taking off his glasses and looking down at me.

The sun is behind him so I can't see his eyes.

'And what's your name?' he sings at me.

I look down at the ground and smile stupidly. I'm not supposed to talk to strangers.

'What's in the box?'

I open the lid.

'Well, what do we have here?'

He sits down on the step next to me. He studies the worms, lifting the leaves to find them all. I blush, proudly maternal.

Then he carefully picks up a zebra.

'He's a beauty.'
What happens next is alarming.
He drops it into his mouth.

He is laughing and I am sitting there looking right into his wet open mouth so that I can see it crawling around on his tongue, head swaying, blindly lost and missing its mulberry leaves, like a cow in a field without grass.

'He needs to go home now,' I say. I feel the anxious concern of a mother who has already known the shame of child neglect.

He closes his mouth and he's still laughing and I am staring at him, waiting for his mouth to open. He shakes his head.

'Oh Goddammit! You should have seen your face!'

'Where's my zebra?'

'Sorry…'

He has swallowed it.

I can't believe it. I am staring at his mouth waiting for him to spit out the zebra. He says, 'Sorry man, it was a mistake, and anyway there are still twelve left and thirteen is an unlucky number for silkworms.'

I am too surprised to cry.

That is my first introduction to Uncle Bryan, my mother's friend, the man my mother is marrying.

Uncle Bryan tries other tricks on us, like the invisible hair and the burnt match one, or the appearing and disappearing penny one. Thomas and I watch him with folded arms and sulk while my mother's laughter tinkles nervously over our heads. Once we see him kissing our mother with his mouth open, the same mouth that swallows worms, sucking the breath from her till she pushed him away all red in the face.

Gaga says Uncle Bryan has 'bedroom eyes' like Clarke Gable. His eyes are certainly a startling blue, and the sun has burnt his skin brown and freckled, but only where his shirt ends at the neck. In his swimming trunks, he looks tan and white like Papa's best shoes, or the two-toned Tamboti bowls you can buy at Mbabane market.

We've seen my mother dance with Uncle Bryan at the hotel in the valley called the Swazi Inn where, once, the big blue swimming pool swallowed me and I sank to the bottom like a stone in a tadpole pond. I watched my life swim away from me in clouds of blue and green, until I discovered the slimy floor with my feet and propelled myself up like a spring and managed to grab onto the ladder. Frightened and exhilarated, I had to find someone to tell because our Mum was in the bar drinking brandy and Coke with the uncle, so I pulled on the sleeve of a passing Swazi waiter.

'I just nearly drowned, hey.'

'Auw! Sorry, Ntombezane.'

He found me a clean white hotel towel and I ordered Coke in a glass with ice and a straw.

My Mum looks like a movie star herself when she is all dressed up and dancing in the hotel lounge. With her shoulders back and head held up high she moves like a Hollywood queen. I think she's beautiful with her black curly hair pinned back, her lips spread red with lipstick and her rouged cheeks. When she dances she looks quite different from the schoolteacher who leaves every morning bent under the weight of books and stolid resignation. As far back as I can remember there has always been an exquisite sadness about my mother, like one of Gaga's porcelain ladies. Dancing with Uncle Bryan seems to make her shine.

'Will we move away from Gaga and Papa's house?' I ask.

'I expect so. You can't live with other people forever.'

I am not prepared for such an abrupt answer; I love it here and I want to live with other people forever. I don't want things to be any different than they are.

We stay on at the old house though, even after they are married, and after a while we do call him Dad, slipping into the habit almost unnoticed.

Our new Dad stays with our Mum for only three months and then heads off to build a dam in Rhodesia, returning at intervals throughout the next year to visit us and to dance with my Mum until her belly grows too big for it.

XIV

I have named all the porcelain and china ladies that live in Gaga's glass display cabinet, wistful English names borrowed from *The Children's Treasure House of Motherland and Empire*. Dame Mary, Lady Agnes, Victoria, Matilda and Petronella. Gaga says all black girls should have English names because their own names are impossible to pronounce. PapaMac says most of them do, the kaffirs have two names in the colonies, their own ones and their adopted ones. Mum says that kaffir is a rude word that shouldn't be spoken out loud and Thomas and I are forbidden to say it, ever. Even though the grown-ups use it from time to time, especially the one that has become our new Dad.

The ladies' porcelain skirts billow in folds from slim waists as though they froze solid at the sudden turn of a winter wind and stayed that way forever.

It's because I am seldom permitted to touch them that a perverse sense of possessiveness grows in me. It is only when Gaga takes them out for dusting that she permits me to stroke them and examine the white bony hands, the cold shod feet and lacy bonnets.

In Gaga's lounge, on a tall table there is a bronze boy who is forever fishing, and I am permitted to engage with him regularly. He's also old and valuable, says my grandmother, but made of much sturdier stuff, not likely to break like the wind-blown ladies. I trace my fingers over the folds of his metal coat, up his neck and along his arm to the rod and down the thin copper wire to the cold scales of the fish balanced on curling waves of hard black bronze. I know every curve and ripple, and in the tips of my fingers I come to understand the shape of it, the tilt of the head, the surprised mouth.

There are other shapes too that I am learning to understand, things in the house and garden that are evident in the drawings that I bring home from school. I am suddenly aware of owning an attribute that has appeared overnight, that has won me unmerited attention and admiration from the grown-ups. Its name is Talent and because it seems quite rare, like being born with twelve toes, and sparingly bestowed on a chosen few, I wear it proudly.

My mother has brought home a box of pencil crayons and a navy blue tin that contains eight colour tablets of water paints and a hog-hair paintbrush. I sit on the veranda floor, half-closing my eyes to see the trees and mountains through the wire netting, dipping and licking the bristles, while my picture takes on muddy shades of brown. A small brown snake zig-zags up the wire netting. I watch his silver belly slide up the vertical length in a deliberate defiance of gravity.

The whole afternoon I wait for him to come down. I imagine him weaving himself in and out of the thatch and climbing down the chimney while we sleep. I draw a snake along the top of a clean page and a girl with a chopper that chops off his head, chip-chop chip-chop last snake's head off. I delight in the idea that you can control and change the outcome of things on paper, using pencils and paintbrushes like the wands of a magician, making things happen and unhappen.

After lots of unhappy mistakes and hours of practice I am learning how to blend the colours so that pure blue and orange and purple shades begin to emerge from my first muddy attempts. You have to keep each tablet completely clean and the brush washed between each change of colour.

Our Uncle Hugh has brought me two sable brushes from Johannesburg and a set of twelve watercolour tubes in a tiny box. I keep them in a Sunrise Toffee box next to my bed, proudly, as they are entirely my own.

Sometimes I see, actually see, the clouds changing, growing moody by the minute from quiet grey to sultry indigo, coaxed by an impending storm. The mountains change hues all day long too, and when the mists roll in they are silhouettes of the softest lilac before they disappear behind the swirling pearly white.

This I know I cannot begin to capture on paper. I just stare beyond the wire mesh or from the steps of the veranda and gape at the changing sky, the silhouettes of the gumtree forests on the mountains, the horizon layered like paper cut-outs.

'Shut your gob, man, you look like a goldfish,' Thomas says.

'It changes colour all the time.'

'What's that got to do with the price of eggs?'

Some things just aren't important in the world of Thomas.

For me, there is another world too, in which I have to find my place. Kindergarten is a foreign place where your shoes squeak in cool corridors and off-by-heart responses drone drearily from chalk-dust classrooms. Here we are managed like an army of small people, and every day seems the same, nose blowing before assembly, numbers and sums and alphabet songs. It is colourless. It is my first introduction to competitiveness among six-year-old girls who are concerned with birthday parties, bride dolls, Kool-Aid verses, and Coca-Cola in their juice-bottles, things that mean nothing in my world.

One day I find my teacher sitting in the lounge, drinking tea.

'What do you say, Gillian?' says Mum.

I say, 'Hello, Miss.'

I perch on the edge of PapaMac's armchair and grin inanely.

'My, don't we look pretty today, all dressed up. What a pretty frock!'

Behind her, Matilda, Petronella and Lady Agnes – the lamenting porcelain ladies – stare out from the windows of the glass cabinet. My mother reminds me that politeness is a disguise that overcomes everything else.

'What do you say, Gillian?'

I say, 'Thank you.'

'Yes, well, as I was saying, I think Gillian should be encouraged to make more of an effort to socialize with the other girls. Perhaps bring a friend home every now and then?' Her hands dance through the air, catching parts of speech like insects. Miss du Toit's nails are perfectly shaped and painted pearl pink. My own are bitten to the quick. I slip them between my dress and the chair and sit on them. Mum is smiling at me, strangely polite, as if she is examining this child for the first time through another's eyes. My mother doesn't ever paint her nails.

Outside the window you can hear the hadedahs laugh. They have settled on the lawn to eat the worms that only they can find.

'Well, she has a birthday coming up. I thought a party...' My mother stumbles headlong into the trap.

'Ah, excellent. A fine idea! The class is by no means too large. I think there are about twelve of you in the class, Gillian?'

My words are perfectly formed on the back of my tongue. No I don't think it is a good idea, and yes there are twelve and I don't want any of them to come. It is my tongue that refuses to throw them out of my mouth. So I shrug an ambiguous answer, while my objection slips away through the soles of my feet. I stare down at my shoes, shining black ones with windows to let your toes breathe. To refuse an adult is bad manners, but shyness is an impediment, like a deformity you're born with. I think most of my peers think I have a speech defect. I am used to watching them from the periphery of their world as if I were the audience to their play. They seem to know the script by heart, the choreography, the body language, the jibe and rebuttal, while I am afflicted with stage fright because the director has forgotten to give me a script. There are two other tribal misfits like me. One is Lorraine, the Portuguese girl whose ears are forever damaged with gold earrings and who has yellow hair that turns green in the summer from the chemicals they put in the public pool. Lorraine struggles bitterly with English and had to stand up in front of the class because she wrote 'human beings' instead of 'Europeans' in a geography test. There are thousands of black people in Swaziland, and all the rest are human beings. Miss du Toit read it out aloud, barely smothering her mirth and it took the class a while to figure out the joke, though in retrospect, I'm sure the irony was lost on all of us.

Sorry Lorraine.

Then there's Rebecca, an unnaturally skinny girl with dark curly hair and nervous eyes she hides behind thick glasses, Four-Eyes-Beck. We are the two best readers in the class, so the two of us swap books and words occasionally.

I am happily invisible, Miss.

I am pinned on the walls in my paintings and drawings.

I get the pencil letters, light up, dark down, slant right, the times and division sums, Egyptian pyramids and spelling Mes-o-pot-amia. Never as exuberant and popular as Thomas, or swaggering with the ease and confidence of Mary-Anne, or tossing thick blonde plaits over my shoulders like Denise Hardy who sticks her tongue out at the boys who follow her around and laugh at her jokes. Though sometimes I wish…

But my mother is concerned about the reluctance with which I face the real world. She assumes all the guilt for my inadequacies. Her daughter is estranged from the society of other little girls, who do normal things. She feels entirely to blame, and shall put matters right to redeem herself.

So the day of my seventh birthday lies in wait like a punishment.

XV

My evening bath time has become a ritual of storytelling and soapsuds. Martha kneels at the edge of the bath with rolled-up sleeves.

'Lie down to wet your hair.'

'Tell me first what the king does with all his warriors at the time of the first fruits.'

Martha protests my blatant bribery, but her delight in the telling of her stories easily overcomes her.

'He sends the young men to take the branches of the Lusekwane trees to bring them at full moon back to Lobamba.'

'But why?'

'Because to make them strong and to make nhlamelo is like a place for King Sobhuza to stay for Incwala. Now you must wet your hair.'

'What happens next?'

'The youngest men go to collect wood branches from the mbondvo. Then they make the place for the king from all the wood. Then all the men come, the chiefs, the elders and they come with the calabash and clay pots with water from the big rivers and the sea. And then King Sobhuza himself arrives. All the warriors begin to sing the Incwala songs. They look very fine.'

'Don't rub so hard, you're hurting me.'

'Put the cloth on your eyes and lie down. That is when they kill the big black ox.'

'But why must they kill it?' She lifts me out and wraps me in a towel, rubbing my skin red.

'You don't ask why things happen in Africa. You ask how.'

'How then?'

'They come closer and closer to the ox and he is crazy with the muti. His eyes are red and he is very angry. Then they hit him with their fists like this.'

She raises her clenched fists and hits the air again and again.

I see the enraged ox lying on his back, the red dust rising towards the face of the moon. He is dizzy with the beating he can no longer bear and the noise of a thousand warriors raging, for no particular reason I could ever understand, but because that was the way things had happened for many years in Africa.

'Is the ox dead now?' I ask.

'Oh yes. He is cut into pieces with the warriors' knives. And all the time the men dance in and out, around a great fire, and they sing praises for the coming of the first fruits. Then they drink beer and the people beg Sobhuza to be their king for one more year.'

'And what does he say?'

'He shakes his head and thinks about it. Then he takes the first fruits of the New Year, the wild pumpkin, and he eats it. Then it starts to rain and Incwala is finished until next year.'

'I am sad for the ox,' I say.

'Psha! The ox is just a man cow, and we kill cows all the time for eating.'

When I ask Martha if she has seen Incwala herself, she laughs.

'Me, I go to the church every Sunday and sing Halleluiahs for

Jesus. The ancestors do not speak to me any more. Now put on your pyjamas yourself.'

At Sunday School they call Jesus a lamb, but the soldiers killed him anyway by hanging him up on a cross with nails and we sing 'All things bright and beautiful', which might have had something to do with 'my soul's as white as snow, now that my sins are washed away'. Soap and cleanliness have a lot to do with God and goodness. My grandmother certainly believes in the redeeming power of soap.

XVI

Our Mum has a tummy the size of a watermelon. It is so heavy that she needs to keep her feet off the ground and rest every afternoon. The house is out of bounds during the day, Gaga says, and we'd better get used to being quiet for when the baby comes.

'When the baby comes' is synonymous for a future change that the grown-ups are more convinced about than I am. But things are already beginning to change at Little Ezulwini. It has been decided that Thomas and I should move into the rondavel behind the kitchen, and our cousin Lally is coming to stay for the holidays. More significant, though, is that, our new Dad will be coming home from Rhodesia for good.

A Swazi girl who reaches the age of six years leaves her mother's khaya for the sake of her parents' privacy. She is now old enough to share a khaya with her sisters, and to take part in the household chores such as sweeping the yard, gathering twigs for the fire and helping generally in her mother's kitchen. She learns the attitude of modesty befitting a young maiden; she learns that subservience to the culture of men is mandatory.

I am six years old and have learnt no such thing.

Perhaps it is because we are now physically separated from the adults that all the night sounds become magnified, and though the stone and cement path between the cottage and the kitchen is only ten yards long, it's an eternal stretch of no-man's-land in the blackness of nightfall.

Thomas is home from boarding school. We are lying in our beds counting the lizards that slither across the black gum-poles and disappear into the thatch. It soon becomes a ritual, a superstition that once begun we dare not break. Counting them keeps them from falling on our heads at night.

'That's eleven. Sleep now.'

'Twelve.'

'We counted that one already. Silly bugger's come back.'

'Twelve.'

'Shuddup and go to sleep.'

The bathroom light is on in the bungalow, a welcome invitation for everything crawling and flying because the window latch is rusted and won't close. That small gap lets in every creature from the garden and the underworld of the African bush. In the morning we must face the daily task of running the taps and watching the whirling water suck the dead powdery moths, spiders and daddy-long-legs into the unknown depths of the plumbing under the white enamel bath. Insects don't belong in baths, they are foreign, intruders, alien things that are uninvited. It isn't as if they have no space outdoors.

Thomas collects the fat black millipedes for dirt races. Thomas isn't afraid of insects like I am. He crushes them, pulls their legs off and shoots at them with a pea-shooter.

I just don't want them to be there, so I close my eyes and drown them when there's no one there to do it for me. I hate the insect bath, but there's comfort in the warm light. It makes the night less menacing, the noises in the dark outside less ominous.

The high-pitched singing of crickets and cicada beetles is holding up the night sky, eagle-owls throw questions at the stars, who? who?, rustling their dry wings amongst the flat paper leaves of the gum-trees, rude bull-frogs burp in the damp underworld, and all the while the natives drum secret messages in the valley.

But one night there is another sound, an anonymous voice from some nameless source.

'Hey, you hear that?' Thomas sits upright.

'I don't want to, Thomas.'

The dog begins to bark in the kitchen yard.

'It's just Ziggie,' I say.

Ziggie is Papa's old Alsatian that he brought from Jo'burg. We have given up trying to get him to play with us, he's ancient, and spends most of his time warming his old joints in a patch of sun near the kitchen door.

'It came from behind the rondavel.'

Thomas leaps out of bed and pushes the back of a chair against the round brass handle of the door because there is no key to lock it from the inside. He peeps through the curtains and stands there for ages peering out into the darkness.

'What is it?'

'Ssssh! D'you hear it?'

I am shivering under the covers, even though the night is warm and balmy enough for no blankets at all.

'What's out there, Thomas?'

'Dunno. Someone or something. Don't worry it can't come in now. I'll stay awake until I know it's gone.'

I have buried my head under the blankets to shut out images of painted warriors and half-beasts that come in the night for children who have to sleep away from the house where the grown-ups live. I am angry with Thomas because his bravery doesn't fool me. I know he is frightened too.

XVII

'Jeeslaik! Look at that!'

We are still in our pyjamas, examining the damp ground at the back of the rondavel.

'Told you 'twasn't a dog,' Thomas says. 'Those are leopard footprints.'

'No, they're not.'

'I swear.'

'How can you tell?'

'They're different from dog prints. Man, look at the size of them!'

'How d'you know it's a leopard?'

'There are spans of leopards in the mountains. They could easily come down here. There aren't any fences to keep them out.'

'I don't want to sleep out here in the rondavel any more.'

But our Mum doesn't care what happens to us in the middle of the night. Our new Dad is sleeping in the big house instead of us, and 'when the baby comes' has changed the way everything used to be. Our Mum's a mother once or twice removed since the Dad came.

The Dad laughs at Thomas when he tells them about the leopard and tells him to grow up, as if we could change the eternal time it takes to make it happen ourselves.

'You'll be afraid of your own shadow next. I don't know any boy your age that's still afraid of the dark.'

My brother's face is burning red. It is me who's afraid of the dark, not him. Thomas isn't even afraid of scorpions, or bats, or snakes. But a wild animal in the garden is another thing altogether, and what could a boy do about that?

Mum has found us a real police whistle from town. 'If anything happens, just blow the whistle as loud as you can and we'll hear you,' she tells us.

'But for heaven's sake, don't just blow it for any old reason. I'm depending on both of you to be sensible, especially you, Thomas. What about when the baby comes? I can't still be worrying about the two of you at night. You're big enough. If you're scared of being alone, I'll ask Martha to move into the rondavel.'

Thomas shrugs off that suggestion.

'We're not scared. We'll be fine.' He glares at me and withers the grimace of protestation from my face.

This is the beginning of Thomas's quest for the phantom leopard. It's more in his head than anywhere else. He begins to read all he can about leopards. He speaks to Solomon and learns about the ancient customs of hunting and the first native warriors who hunted leopards on the plains and in the mountains of Swaziland. He writes down pages of information, taken from encyclopaedias and library books. He carefully pencils the words in thin exercise books, cuts them out neatly and pastes them in a scrapbook.

Thomas has traced the paw prints we found on the ground in pencil on wax paper before the next rains come.

I have traced the outline of a crouching lioness from a colouring book and coloured it with black spots that look like the flower patterns on a leopard's back. I have given it to Thomas and he has stuck it into his scrapbook after The History of Leopards.

He's also pasted magazine pictures and postcards after the part about grinding whiskers for muti.

I have become a faithful consort in my brother's new pursuit. I sometimes wake up in the night to find Thomas sitting at the window, staring into the darkness through a crack in the curtains, waiting. I wonder if he ever sleeps at all.

'Did you hear it, Thomas?'

He shakes his head and puts his hand up for me to be quiet, as if he knows it is out there listening for us. Strangely enough, I am no longer afraid. I'm as keen as my brother for a nightly visit. It never crosses my mind to ask Thomas if and when he has actually seen the leopard. The way he describes it, imagined or real, I almost begin to believe that I have seen it myself.

I still have Thomas's scrapbook with the neat pages of writing in pencil, along with the tracings of leopard spoor and the childish copy of the colouring book lioness that I disguised with spots, like floral wallpaper. It is ironic that I should be the one who completes this story, and with the same obsessive drive that once was his.

PART TWO

Rahab

I dreamt again that I lost you to the leopard. I woke up whimpering like a child.

I hate that moment of waking and meeting the strange partaker of your dreams, finding a hysterical stranger in the sanctity of your bed. In my dreams I am desperately looking for you, running past tables laden with raw and bloody meat served on platters of white porcelain. I am alone. Everything is grey, like the early evening light of an overcast day. Above me is the constant flutter of dark wings, black birds outside the window, above my reach. How can sound be so loud in a dream? There are passages that lead into vast rooms, but no doors to the garden, and I know you are out there on the hill.

I look down at my feet. They are small as a child's, running on a thick carpet patterned in red and gold and black, an oriental design with an intricate weave. The patterns merge into black rosettes on a back of gold. The carpet begins to heave. The shape of a leopard emerges, the eyes of the Watcher. She has come back.

I cannot see her face. She is moving away from me, crouching in stealth like the hunter she is. She has come to take you. I know this, but I cannot run any more. I can't stop her, I am weak and helpless, a child again, caught up in dreams that have nothing to do with real things.

I float up, moth-like, towards the ceiling where the lizards live. All my prayers and wishes are written on postage stamps stuck on the gum posts or caught in the thatch. None of them made their way to heaven after all.

Two years ago, in the bright neon light of an early morning kitchen, after a night haunted by these dreams, I started scribbling – reaching backwards over a span of fifty years of forgetting, trying to summon the elusive details that had faded with neglect like a story you hear once and never again.

I wrote in the evening or early morning when the house was still with sleep, picking through the threads of a memory unreliable and fragmented, trying to separate the real from the imagined.

I also took to sketching leopards.

The creature that I drew was a presence, powerful and solitary, often seen through a doorway, a window, rising up from a hiding place, at once beautiful and menacing. I worked on large sheets of paper, discarding most of them on the floor. It wasn't accuracy I sought. It was that elusive presence. The power in her beautiful flanks, the arch of her back, the movement of force in that neck. At times she was trapped in a charcoal prison of architecture, straining for her release. On one page her face moves in staccato images from stillness to anguish, mouth open, a strangely contorted neck. As I came to feel her presence in the form of my drawings I began not only to remember more vividly, but to feel the memory like a released fragrance. I knew that it was time to go back.

I had to understand the mystery of this beast, what she became for Thomas from the time we first heard her and found her tracks on the damp soil outside the rondavel. Then later the betrayal, and the disbelief, seeing her lying there that morning on the cement porch, blood stained, mouth open and slack. It strikes me now – that was the first time I actually saw her.

It was Thomas who knew her and followed her. He was the only one.

II

Up here, towards the west and beyond the rhyolite rocks, you can see the tall peaks of the Swaziland highlands, vague silhouettes hardly visible. Below these mountain crags is the wide Sispiso valley, a sea of thick grass interspersed with termite mounds like scattered sleeping sheep, and grey thorn shrubs. And below us, on the eastern side, the ironwood forest.

If she is royalty, if she is queen then we are her subjects, diminished by our vulnerable human status. We are of little consequence to her. No threat she now knows, and no prey, just curious spectators burdened with inanimate machines that click and zoom and whine above the sounds of insects and birds on the air.

I sit on the outskirts of this theatre watching and drawing. In the quiet of this place graphite on paper becomes a sound that alludes to presence like a tail's swish, a muzzle's quiver. Wild is silent. Noise is understated for prey and predator alike. I watch my own hand deftly sketch the form of her.

My sketches have progressed from gesture and the study of skeletal and muscle structure to the finer details, facial expression and the distinctive markings on her coat. The rosettes seem quite arbitrary at first but on closer examination, they are patterned to the rhythms and contours of her body and face. From her cheekbones to the edges of her mouth there is a dramatic gradation from straw colour to a dense black. It accentuates the sudden scarlet flesh of her open mouth.

I am coming to know her, to be her. Drawing is like that. A photograph captures a moment, an immediacy that is fleeting; the art of drawing is a process that allows the form to grow gradually through soft strokes of pencil like touching, like feeling. Shape and texture. Know this intimately, a slow shy dance moving into another's space, touching the flesh with the eyes' caress, listening to the sound of the soul.

I wonder how Thomas felt the moment he came face to face with her up there on the mountain. He was never afraid. Or was he? Is this how he saw her?

Here in the sun her coat is gold, patterned rust and black with a necklace of black at her throat on clean white fur that strokes down to her belly. The black is so black it drinks in the light like burn holes. In the shade she is dappled bronze, shadow fragments, part of a tree, or leafy shade spilling out under a rock ledge. Camouflage. Her beauty is her hiding place. Who would expect the shape she becomes, rising from the gentle play of light and shade in the leaves? And from that shape, languid and lovely? In the lazy white-sun days she seems indolent, apathetic, but if you were deceived by her apparent indifference, then you would be a fool.

III

Our stepfather has brought his guns down from Rhodesia. He likes to take them out and clean them at the weekends like a ceremony. He has two rifles, a shotgun and a pistol. The smaller calibre .22 rifle is an effective weapon for hunting springbok and other smaller game, he says.

The larger one, a .306, is for more serious shooting.

'This is a hunter's best friend, if he's a good shot. It'll take out an eland, a kudu, even a lion – as long as you aim for the heart,' he says.

He holds out four rocket-shaped lead-tipped bullets on the palm of his hand. He lets Thomas hold one and he rolls it in his fingers, feels its weight, its awesome significance. Thomas grins.

'You can't afford to miss even once with a lion, not with a rifle.

Otherwise you just wound him and then you're asking for bloody trouble.'

He aims at the surprised fisher boy through the sights and slowly squeezes the trigger. Thomas is entirely captured by this game.

'Now, the shotgun is effective for hunting a variety of game. Twelve bore. See these slugs?'

They look like giant firecrackers, a roll of 3X Mints. He reaches out, takes my hand and rolls one into my palm.

'Quite heavy, huh?'

He lifts me onto his lap.

'Each one of these contains small lead bullets. Have to be close up if you're using this on big game.'

'Even an elephant?' I say, watching his hands stroke the barrel. His hands are big and rough. The Dad is brave and strong enough to protect us from anything. I want to lay my head against his hard chest where the suntan ends at the first button of his shirt. But I don't. I leave his lap and sit on the floor at his feet.

After taking them apart he shoves the metal cleaning rod tipped with soft chamois leather down the barrels, and greases the working parts tenderly with his thick tobacco-stained fingers. The lounge is sour with the smell of gun oil and metal. He stops now and then and sips from a glass of whisky and lights a cigarette that he bites between his teeth while he works. Then he polishes the wooden butts with a rag until they shine in the lamplight. It is a careful and deliberate procedure that inspires awe and respect from his audience.

The Dad really loves his guns. I only ever saw that same reverence on the face of my grandmother as she dusted and stroked her porcelain ladies that live in the glass cabinet.

My mother isn't happy about the guns. You can see it in the way she tightens her lips and the flicker of doubt that moves across her eyes like a shadow when the Dad unlocks the stinkwood cupboard in the lounge and takes them out. She finally agrees that Thomas be allowed to hold one, unloaded of course, and to look through the sights as if aiming for a buck or a wild hare.

The Dad says his father bought him his first gun when he was eight years old. He says he'll teach Thomas how to shoot and take him hunting one day. I say that I'll go too, but Mum whisks me off to the kitchen to help her make the tea. She says it's men's business, having to do with guns and knives and things, hunting wild animals and rough stuff that excludes girls.

Even though our Mum has never changed her mind about the guns, she seems satisfied that Thomas is learning men's business from our new Dad and Thomas seems pleased too. The importance of these lessons mitigates the quiet insinuation of malevolence that comes to live with the porcelain ladies in Gaga's lounge.

The Dad shows us photographs of the time in Rhodesia when they were saving the animals before the Zambezi dam water came. Most of them drowned, he says. They had to save what they could. They caught buck, rhinos, even snakes, and took them to higher ground. 'Operation Noah' it was called; saving the animals from the flood just like the Bible story except there were lots of Noahs and the boats that they used when the waters started rising were small motorboats with engines on the back.

We are sitting on the carpet in the lounge around a box of the Dad's photographs. There are faded old photos of a little boy with blonde curls sitting on a horse, the same child sitting in a huge basket of oranges, another one of the child laughing broadly at the camera from the generous lap of a young woman, the same boy with his hair cut short, holding a shotgun at his side, looking straight ahead with a solemn expression as if he'd suddenly grown up.

There are lots of pictures of the Dad driving a jeep through the bush in Rhodesia, hauling animals into a boat out of the rising water, standing around with other men in khaki, all of them carrying shotguns and looking immensely satisfied. There are pictures of animals too, with hunters standing over them beaming into the camera, proudly holding onto the horns of a buck or, in one picture, the mane of a huge lion. There are also photographs of motorboats and canoes with drugged animals being hauled on and off by game wardens, their limbs clumsy and awkward with sleep.

I see Thomas look up at the Dad like there is something different about the way he sees him. Then he comes out with it.

'Do you have any photos of leopards, Dad?'

It is the first time I've heard my brother call him that.

The Dad pulls out another box, pours himself another drink and the two of them sit on the couch like an exclusive men's club.

That night, when we climb into bed, and when Thomas has written another entry into his book, he says he's found a name for our leopard.

'What is it?'

'It's Shaba. Dad knew a leopard called Shaba once. In Rhodesia. It got stuck on an island in the middle of the lake for two whole months. It was too far from the mainland to swim, so it lived on fish and crabs. Just imagine, hey! But don't tell anyone, OK? I don't want him to know that I borrowed the name from him.'

'It's a good name, Thomas.'

Now it has a name, it has really become our own.

Just like the new Dad.

Thomas's next entries in the scrapbook are interspersed with the Dad's photographs of leopards and hunters in Rhodesia. Later, he must have found pictures of guns from the *Farmer's Weekly*. He stuck them in, with meticulous descriptions of make, velocity, calibre and effectiveness.

IV

My cousin Lally has told us that our Gaga has a sixth sense, which means she sees things that normal people like us don't.

'My Ma says it's wrong to see ghosts – it's against the Holy Bible,' she says.

'How's it wrong? Maybe she just can't help it,' says Thomas.

'It's an Irish curse.'

'What ghosts?' I ask. Ghosts don't exist, according to Mum and Mum's a school teacher so she should know better than Lally's mother who stays at home all day painting her nails. I heard Gaga say that once to PapaMac.

Our cousin aspires to royalty and is an ardent fan of the British royal family.

Lally's arrival, coinciding as it does with the time of 'when the baby comes' and the naming of Shaba, is an intrusion we could do without. She is immediately absorbed into my mother's preoccupation with baby things, something I have refused to involve myself in.

Lally has further alienated herself from my brother and me with her blatant disregard for the story about the leopard.

'I'll believe it when I see it for myself,' she says. Even I know that isn't very likely.

As for the name Thomas has chosen for our leopard, at least we have kept that from her.

One morning Thomas walks into the kitchen and asks our Mum if Martha could pack us some sandwiches and orange squash for a picnic lunch.

'The three of us are going for a walk up the hill.'

We often take walks up the hill to the far edge of the granite slopes that look over the valley. Thomas always leads the way, stamping the ground along the path to let the snakes know we are coming. Of course Thomas always turns over the stones to find scorpions. He does it carefully and puts the scorpions in a tin so that he can watch them sting each other to death. They usually just lie there though, frozen in dusty stillness, until we get bored and throw them away.

This time, though, Thomas examines the ground all the way for leopard tracks, and Lally becomes impatient. She takes the lead and stomps her way up the path until she and I arrive at Flat Rock. From up here, where the grass is tall and acacias and cabbage trees grow amongst the granite boulders, we can survey almost the entire kingdom of Swaziland, the faded lilac mountains in the distance, the endless forests of gum trees that sweep down to the lush green of Ezulwini valley. Down there is the thatched roof of Swazi Inn with its blue pool the size of a postage stamp and the distant farmhouses that look as small as monopoly pieces.

Lally pulls three plastic juice bottles out of the leather satchel and props them up in a shaded fissure between two rocks.

'Hey, Thomas, when you going to give up on your leopard?' she shouts. Lally is by far the bossiest and the loudest girl I know.

Thomas ignores her. He's brought his tracing paper just in case he comes across another footprint. He looks up at the mountain behind us, shading his eyes from the glare of the sun. All across the horizon the sun has bleached the sky a faded blue and the distant mountains look almost transparent in the haze.

We have just started unwrapping our jam sandwiches when Lally starts telling us about the black birds.

'When someone is going to die, black birds come into the house, that's what my Daddy told me.'

'I don't believe you,' I say.

I look up at my brother. He's still staring at the mountain.

'It's true. I saw the birds once,' Thomas says.

Lally stops chewing and gawks at him.

'It was when Mum had just left our real father the first time. Gaga and PapaMac came to visit us in Jo'burg the one day and Mum had a black eye. The side of her face was swollen. She tried to make excuses like she always had, but they saw through it. They knew my Dad was beating her. They knew he was a blurrie drunk.'

Now it's my turn to stop chewing and stare. This is what shame feels like. He is talking about someone else's father, not the one I have painted a picture of in my head, forever established like an automatic wind-up cartoon, wandering about a foggy London going nowhere in particular. I sit there dumbly and say nothing because I don't want my cousin to think I don't know, that I don't remember.

Thomas picks up a stick and lobs off the heads of the wild grass.

'What did PapaMac say to your Dad?' Lally asks, her eyes fixed in a wild stare.

'Dad wasn't there. They just made her pack a suitcase and we all left in a hurry and drove all the way to Swaziland.

'The three of us slept in one room. Uncle Hugh was home for the holidays. It was a pretty awful time, Mum was always crying.'

'And the birds?'

'PapaMac's heart was giving him trouble. Mum says he's always had a bad heart. We were sitting on the lawn, Uncle Hugh, Jilly and me. Uncle Hugh is my absolutely favourite person. He's always funny. He can tell a story and take you right into it. I'm going to be just like that some day, excepting that I'll never be a teacher. I'm going to an acting academy overseas.'

'What happened anyway?' Lal says, redirecting the story impatiently.

'He told me something while we were sitting there about the birds. Something like – Papa's had this before, you know, and Gaga's a little fey about things like this. It's the Irish in her. She'll be closing all the windows to keep out the birds. She's convinced that if one of them comes in, he'll be a gonner, for sure. I asked him if he believed in all that stuff, and he laughed.'

'And was it true?' Lally insists.

'When we got back to the house, the windows were all shut tight, and Mum whispered to us that they were to stay that way. No outside doors were to be opened unless by a grown-up, and then they had to be shut immediately.'

'Did you ask her why?'

Thomas laughed wickedly.

'Course I did. You know what it's like; nobody tells us anything. It's something in the air, she said. PapaMac's having trouble breathing in all that grass pollen blown down from the mountain.'

'Did you say anything?'

'Uh-uh, I sat on my bed and read for the rest of the day. Jilly went to sleep.'

'I don't remember,' I interrupt, squeezing my eyes shut tight to see if I could find the elusive memory, but it has fallen off the back edge of my mind into nothingness. 'Then at about five that afternoon Gaga comes running out of her bedroom in a panic. She calls Mum and they both disappear into the bedroom. Mum rushes out again and calls Uncle Hugh. He grabs a broom and goes out into the garden and when I look outside our bedroom window there he is, waving a broom up towards PapaMac's bedroom window. He's shouting and waving frantically.'

'There were birds there?'

'Pecking at the bedroom window, twenty or more of them.'

'You telling the truth, Thomas?'

'I swear. The black birds scattered all of a sudden. They swooped over Uncle Hugh's head and flew up into the sky.'

'Is this just another story, Thomas, 'cause I'll tell on you if you're lying?' says Lal.

'Cross my heart an' hope to die.'

'Oh God, it's so weird.' Lally hugs her knees and grins.

'When Uncle Hugh came into the house his face was white as a sheet. He didn't look at me. He just walked straight into his father's bedroom and shut the door. And of course PapaMac lived on, strong as an ox.'

'I knew it was true,' says Lally.

'No you didn't.'

'Course I did.'

I say: 'I don't remember' – a needle stuck in the groove of a gramophone record. I am not sure whether to believe my brother or not. When it comes to telling stories, real or imagined, Thomas was even better than Martha.

For some reason this shared phenomenon has transformed the animosity between Thomas and Lally into a conspiratorial allegiance that no longer includes me.

Lally has suddenly become animated about the leopard, and the name that Thomas and I have concealed together is soon out in the open. I am the outsider once again, a third wheel on the margin.

This exclusive liaison lasts throughout the holidays and I find myself returning to the isolation I am used to.

V

The late afternoon is wearing a thick shawl of fog, the house is an island floating adrift without a landscape. You cannot hear the rain, only the incessant dripping from the thatch eaves.

On gloomy days the passage is a long airless cupboard. The

scent of my grandmother's eau-de-toilette has found its way from her bedroom and now hangs in dubious company with the wet-dog smell of the damp bathroom carpet I flooded a week ago. The passage carpet is thick and soft beneath bare feet used to rougher outdoor turf. I am forced to tiptoe along the edge nearest the wall so the floorboards don't creak, careful not to wake my sleeping mother. I stop at her door to listen.

Her even breathing assures me that all is well.

I reach up for the passage door handle and open the interleading door to the front hall. I like being alone in this grown-up place, breathing in the quiet of rooms that smell of wax polish, Imbuia and Kiaat and old things with an indefinable scent of their own. The rhythm of the grandfather clock measures each day with ticking, consistent, dependable.

I stop at the window. The driveway and the rockery are gone, swallowed up in white mist. I reach up to trace my fingers over the cold black bronze statue of a naked woman I am sure is my mother. I bathed with my mother once and immediately recognized the very same form that stretches up now beneath my fingers. It doesn't seem at all unusual that Mum's naked self is standing in the hall, arms lifted gracefully above her head, face tilted slightly as if to beckon the rare visitors that come through the front door.

'What are you doing in here?'

My grandmother's voice knifes through the stillness.

My fingers drop behind my back. I am afraid of her quick temper. She takes my hand firmly in hers and leads me back down the passage and into her bedroom. I am trying to remember to breathe. She makes me stand at the foot of her bed and turns the key in her sturdy wooden kist. As she opens it the room is filled with the smell of mothballs. She pulls out a bundle of something wrapped in tissue paper, beckons me to sit on the edge of the bed while she carefully unwraps the parcel.

It is a doll I have never seen the likes of before, with a stone white porcelain face and staring glass eyes.

'Do you want to hold her?' she asks.

Lally's words echo in my head:

My ma says it's wrong to see ghosts – it's against the Holy Bible. But my grandmother's bitter-tight bird-beak lips have given way to a gentle smile. There is a sweetness in her eyes I do not know.

'Careful now. Don't drop her. She came all the way from Paris and she's very old.'

I trace my fingers gently over the small cold face, touching the pretty glass-stone earrings and stroking her yellow silk dress and blue velvet bodice, the soft gold hair. I am afraid of dropping her.

There is a label attached to her ankle, just above the minute kid leather shoes.

'Is it her name?' I whisper.

'It says Jumeau Bisque – Rue Lafitte, Francaise. My mother bought it for me when I was a girl. She's pretty, isn't she?'

'She's an olden-day doll.'

'She's French and very fashionably dressed for her day.'

'I never saw a doll like her before.'

I am sitting so close to Gaga I can smell Yardley's lavender talc wafting from her bosom. Her crisp satin blouse whispers when she moves. I blush with shyness and pleasure.

'That's enough.' Gaga takes the doll from me and wraps her up in the pink tissue paper and restores her to her bed in the mothball kist.

The magical moment has passed, but not before I have a fleeting glimpse of my grandmother's vulnerability. It becomes our secret. In rare moments of generosity she lets me hold the doll and then puts her away, like the porcelain ladies in the display cabinet.

Later I am allowed occasional peeks into the rest of the kist's coveted treasures. This limited access to what is most precious and fragile invokes in me a reverence for obscure icons of antiquity. Gaga's chest of hidden possessions is a cathedral of barely consummated desire that keeps one unsatisfied and wanting more.

I am unsure of the boundaries of my new relationship with my grandmother. She finds me and indulges me at moments when I least expect it. She gets an idea into her head and leads me into a new experience that isn't always to my advantage. Like the time she ties rags into my damp limp hair and insists that I sleep in the twisted screws of linen ribbons. For the sake of feminine tresses, a crowning glory, I endure a torturous night. In the morning she unwraps my hair carefully. The relief is immense, but she is disappointed with the results and so am I.

'It was supposed to come out as pretty ringlets!' she wails. In the mirror my face is framed in a halo of dented frizz. I think of Lally's soft blonde curls and I have to cry. That's a mistake. Gaga is not enamoured with outbursts of tears. She sends me to the bathroom to wash away the unhappy experiment and returns to her kitchen in a sour mood to orchestrate the dinner.

Sometimes I find a silk nightdress, knitted bed socks or a velvet cloak and hood, neatly folded and waiting for me at the end of my bed. She has made them herself, with perfect tucks and ribboned edges. She isn't comfortable with gushes of gratitude; a subtle smile between us is enough and no one else will be party to our shared place of affections. It is some time later that I begin to reciprocate, with the one thing that I am able to give her – the humble fruits of my talent. I choose the best of my drawings and paintings and leave them like offerings on the end of her bed.

It is no use trying to use this new-found favour with my grandmother, even to gain privileged access to cake or biscuits at tea. That is not part of the game. She turns her back on me as if, when the others are around, I am the same nuisance child I have always been.

'Martha, take that child out of the kitchen. What's she doing in the house?'

Our relationship is a mystery.

VI

I spend my days drawing trees with blue sky windows between the branches. Black birds try to fly through the windows, but I can't and won't let them; in my pictures I have the power to change things. When the rain stops and the garden returns, slipping back quietly out of the mist and settling into its former comfortable arrangement like a great big bird returning to ground from its winter migration, I run outside and welcome it back like a lost friend.

In the garden I can choose to be a cowboy, galloping wildly on the backs of invisible horses around the sodden lawns, a Swazi warrior marching to the king's kraal, or captain of my coal-house ship, barking orders at the sailors like my grandmother does with the servants. I rarely choose the roles of female protagonists; there is no adventure in playing out the mundane dramas of domesticity. History has little place for women advancing on undiscovered lands. Men make the rules and win the wars.

Thomas and Lally have become swarthy adventurers joined in secrets and whispered collaboration. They are hellbent on turning over every clue that might bring them closer to the habits of a phantom leopard. I have petulantly decided that there never was a leopard at all and have trashed the idea along with the lies about the black birds and the ghosts. I've tested these unlikely stories on Martha and she has dismissed them like bothersome flies with a wave of her hand. I am greatly comforted.

'Mustn't talk about these things, Miss Jilly. All nonsense talk.'

'What about the leopard? Do you think there really is a leopard?'

'On the mountains far, far from here, there are leopards. But here, it is only the spirit of the leopard that comes and sits in Master Thomas's head.'

'That's what I think.'

Is my brother a liar or an aspiring film star with a huge imagination? Too much imagination gets people into trouble, Mum says.

'My people say that the footprints of a lion you must not follow for he will find you. Thomas must know this,' says Martha.

Martha takes me up the garden to the whitewashed compound where the servants live, to see the new second-hand car that Solomon's brother, Moses, has driven up from Durban. Moses is a smart black man in a city suit and a thin red tie. Moses is no longer a warrior who marches for the king; he is too busy making business in the city, like a white man.

Moses helps Solomon to trim the dagga leaves that grow at the back in an untidy tangle with baboon-tail grass and khaki weed. Solomon likes to roll dry dagga in newspaper and smoke it on a Sunday for his weekend headache. He says it works better than 'Grandpa Headache Powder'. I am not sure if it is my grandpa's powder or not, but I have heard the Dad say that it's the dagga that makes the kaffirs stupid.

Sometimes Solomon cooks up a pot of sorghum beer on the sticks and stones fireplace on the side of the compound where Martha makes tea and cooks their putu for supper. I had a taste of the beer once. It was bittersweet and I liked it. But Thomas said that the blacks cook insects and worms in their beer. I don't believe him, but I will never taste it again. Just in case.

Solomon used to keep a dog at the compound. He didn't bother to give it a name, so Thomas christened it 'Newspaper' on account of his being black and white and grey-smudged with soot. Newspaper disappeared one night, which was just as well, Martha said, because the dog was stealing the servants' chickens, the ones that were free to peck about in the dirt outside the compound. Sometimes the chickens get drunk on the sorghum mush if Solomon leaves it in the pot when the beer is finished. The brown laying chickens in the wire mesh sheds look on in astonishment at their sisters' rocking and rolling in the dust, lifting their feathers and making eyes at the only cock in the coop.

Martha says, 'Auw! You see, it's the beer that makes people stupid.'

Moses' car is jazzed up with neat strips of coloured carpet, even on the dashboard. A plastic Kewpie doll hangs on a string from his mirror, along with a necklace made of coloured glass beads and a cowhide bangle. He has wired up a transistor radio to the front panel and Elvis Presley croons a song about blue suede shoes. This is nothing like Mum's mint-green Morris-Minor we call Angus, or Papa's new Pontiac – a black and silver lounge for six with leather seats and ashtrays – which makes you carsick on long trips to Jo'burg or Durban.

They are all talking and laughing together in a language that I don't understand. Martha is clapping her hands and laughing between yelling at Moses and Solomon as if they are on the other side of the garden. I heard Papa say once that kaffirs don't understand about quiet conversation. He said it is the result of shouting to each other from khaya to khaya across the valleys. It's because they don't have telephones that they have to shout across the valleys. That's why they are standing around the new second-hand car shouting at each other. They aren't angry at all, I remind myself, because they are laughing and clapping and banging on the bonnet to punctuate their sentences.

When Martha walks me back to the house she tells me that Moses will bring her daughter from Durban next time.

'Is she like me?' I say hopefully.

Martha grins widely.

'Look at me, Miss Jilly. I am this old and so my girl is this big.' She slices the air above her head.

'What's her name?'

'Rahab. You know the story of Rahab?'

'No.'

'Then one day I'm telling you this.'

VII

The Rahab you find in the Bible is a beautiful woman called a harlot, who lives in an apartment on the edge of a walled city that stands in a desert as far away from anything you could imagine to do with our life in Swaziland. What is unusual about the story is that she belonged to the wrong side to start with, but she was the one who was saved when the walls came tumbling down, along with her whole family, and she turned out to be a sort of olden day heroine.

When the real Rahab arrives she is not at all what I expect. Although Martha assured me more than once that she was tall and grown up, I still imagined her younger, more like my cousin Lally.

But she is beautiful. She wears her hair in tiny plaits close to her head and pulled into a tight knot at the top. Under a fringe of delicate glass beads that touch her forehead, her dark eyes are bovine, huge and lovely. Her skirts are brightly coloured and tied in layers around her waist, and she wears a floral cloth like a cloak knotted neatly on one shoulder. The holes in her ears are wide and plugged with beaded wheels as big as coat buttons. Martha says that the ears of a child must be pierced so that the ears of the mind can also hear.

Lorraine at school whose father has the fish and chip shop in Mbabane has holes in her ears with little gold hoops in them, but my mother says that body piercing is self-mutilation, which means damaged. I have often wondered why Lorraine has no friends. She is not only Portuguese and a Catholic, which makes her different from everyone else, but now I know she is also damaged. As for all the thousands of Swazis and Zulus, it is a thought that revolves in my own mind until the answer comes to me one day: the ears of their minds are open to things that white people like us cannot understand. That's what makes them different.

Around Rahab's neck is a stiff beaded collar and below that her bare breasts tremble as she walks. She knows only one sentence in English and it seems as if she's learnt it off by heart like an idiom:

'Yes-'m-thank-you-'m.'

She tumbles the words together like one, and curtsies deeply when she speaks, eyes downcast shyly. Her movements are careful and unhurried. I feel a surge of emotion in my chest, not unlike the devotion I feel towards Gaga's porcelain treasures, only more intense. I am standing at the feet of a real storybook princess. Awestruck.

On her feet she wears bright white takkies, bought at the trading store in Empangeni, Martha told me, especially for the journey. Martha is wailing with excitement, tears flowing from her eyes in an endless stream, running into her smiling mouth and down her chin. I stand back, embarrassed. I understand little of what is said, but gather that she is thanking Moses, who leans over the bonnet of his blue second-hand car, smoking a cigarette. Like tennis ball banter, loud shouting is bounced to and fro, and a lot of clicking sounds in between. Then Martha dismisses both Solomon and Moses with a wave of her hand, to which the men respond with loud guffaws of laughter. Martha grabs my hand and gestures for her daughter to follow us to her compound khaya.

Martha has never let me into her khaya before, but now that she is sleeping at the foot of my bed because Thomas is away at boarding school, she has arranged her room especially for her daughter's visit. The compound is made up of four rooms in a row. Precious lives in the room next to Martha and then there's a storeroom filled with Papa's gardening stuff, and Solomon's room is on the end. The rain has licked up red soil stains on the whitewashed walls. The front yard is a dirt and scrub lawn where white chickens scatter sideways and eye us with hardy suspicion. It has been swept clean so often that the topsoil has long since disappeared. No grass grows here, only at the back where the wild grass, khaki weed and dagga grow in happy companionship with the nesting chickens.

Martha's door has a broken latch, so there's a brick on the inside to keep it shut. The room is dark because there's no electricity in the compound, and the window is small and covered with a red and white checked curtain. When your eyes have adjusted to the dark interior from the bright sunlight outside, you can see that the walls are papered with magazine and newspaper pages to keep out the damp and cold. Shelves on the wall are laden with blackened aluminium pots of various sizes and an assortment of biscuit tins that stand neatly stacked on one side. A small painted table carries a kerosene lamp, a candle, matches and a well-worn leather-bound Bible.

In one corner there is a long pine box with badly fitted shelves that serves as a clothes cupboard. On hangers that swing from a hook on the wall Martha's 'smart' clothes wait for Sunday church or town visits on her afternoon off. The iron bed, neatly made with an assortment of blankets and rugs, is hoisted up on bricks as is the custom, to keep out the mischief of the Tokoloshe, that dwarf beast, half man and half animal, that takes any opportunity to slip into a bedroom unnoticed.

Tokoloshe is a sad little beast whose evil comes from the sorcerer who used him to hide objects filled with 'muties' in dark hiding places to cast spells on the black people. He is the African goblin: a hairy creature with hands and feet as small as a monkey, with a penis rudely long and pointed like a tail. Thomas, Lally and I have seen the black piccaninnies from the 'location' across the hill, swimming in the farm dam, their black bodies thin and wiry and their thingies protruding astonishingly long like hosepipes from their fronts. That is how I imagine the Tokoloshe, except he is short and squat like a monkey.

'Can't the Tokoloshe reach you if you make your bed stand on bricks?'

She laughed. 'It's so that it's not dark under and we can see the mutie that he leaves there hidden in the horn of the cow, the box of matches and the what-what. We sweep clean every day, and let the light in.'

I thought about the underneath of my own bed, shadowed in a dark uncertainty that I wouldn't dare investigate.

'Will he ever hide things under my bed?'

Martha pulled my face close to her own.

'You pray every night to the Lord Jesus that nothing will come into your room, Miss Jilly. Though I walk through the valley of death, I will fear no evil. Remember this.'

Rahab pulls her basket into the room and stands shyly at the door. Martha is giving her instructions about the lamp, the cupboard and the pots on the shelf. She pulls down the biscuit tins and opens them one by one, sugar, tealeaves in a small caddy, ideal milk and salt. Then in another, an assortment of creams, Zambuck, toothpaste, Ponds Vanishing Cream and lipice, and two bars of red Lifebuoy soap.

Rahab smiles all the time. She touches all Martha's things shyly as if she is stroking the mother in them.

Rahab cannot leave the compound because my grandmother does not approve of tribal dress anywhere near the house.

'I will not have savages in my house or garden,' she told PapaMac, when she caught sight of Solomon returning from a celebration, dressed in his tribal regalia. 'There's no excuse for bringing their dark and primitive ways anywhere near the house. I will not have them dressed in skins and feathers on my property.'

As long as she stays up at the compound, it is acceptable that Martha's daughter should be dressed as a 'heathen'. The compound is not visible from the house. It is situated at the very top of the garden, behind the chicken coop and overgrown lantana bushes and red-hot-pokers.

Every day for the rest of the week, Martha takes me, along with some of her household chores, up to the compound so that she can sit with Rahab and talk. I sit with them and listen to the rhythmic music of the Zulu language. Moses has decided to stay for the week, and PapaMac says he could use the extra help. He has acquired a steel contraption to make cement bricks to build a wall between our garden and the road.

In the afternoons Solomon and Moses mix cement and turn out bricks one at a time, laying them out in neat rows to dry in the sun. They work at the top of the garden from where they can see the three of us sitting under the tree, shelling peas, peeling vegetables or scrubbing washing in the zinc tub. Conversation is a loud ball game thrown to and fro and I am the piggy-in-the-middle watching the words rise and fall like pictures with wings, a Zulu drama with laughter and hand gestures, reproaches and observations. I am the uncomprehending audience trying to read between the lines.

Then one afternoon the Dad comes home early from the pineapple factory and walks in his brisk fashion up the garden path to examine the brick-making project. Martha and I are shelling peas. It is a job I love to do, popping the crisp pods and scooping the tight, hard peas into the bowl, biting into the odd sweet one that escapes into my mouth.

Rahab is rinsing clothes in a tin bucket at the tap, up to her elbows in water, her bare breasts jiggling under her beaded collar. I see the Dad stand up stock-still and stare in our direction. He shouts across to me:

'What are you up to, Gillian?'

'Nothing.'

He starts walking towards us and then stops and stares at Rahab who is still plunging her elbows in the bucket. Martha says something to her and Rahab looks up and smiles shyly at the Dad. I can hardly describe the look that comes upon his face then. His mouth turns up under his moustache and I am sure it is a smile forming, but it turns into a grimace that most closely resembles disgust.

The Dad throws sharp words at Martha in her language and my nanny casts her eyes towards the ground, her lips stiffening in a straight line. She shakes her head and remains silent.

'Put. That. Stuff. Down,' he says to me.

He grabs my arm and pulls me to my feet and I watch stray peas roll away from me like green tears onto the dust. He pushes me ahead of him in the small of my back so that I stumble down the stone path towards the house.

'Don't let me catch you hanging about with the kaffirs at the compound again.' His voice barks over my head. 'God knows what kind of germs you could pick up!'

I start walking towards the kitchen.

'I want my mother,' I say.

He grips my arm again, almost lifting me off the ground. It's hurting. He pushes his face into mine; I can smell stale cigarettes in his words.

'Don't you understand? How can you even think of bringing that filth anywhere near the baby. Look at your feet! Go to the rondavel and run a bath. You're big enough to bath yourself.' He lets go of me suddenly so that I stumble in an effort to keep my balance.

My tears are still stuck and burning at the back of my throat like lemon pips as I stand above the bath and watch the insects float on the rush of water and swirl down the plughole. It is the ones that won't go with the flow, the ones that keep climbing back up, that refuse to drown, that I hate the most. I measure the extent of my misery by listing all the things that are changing in my life, like the insects that I am drowning one by one. It goes like this:

This one's the Dad who has come home to stay like a nightmare and lied about me being his special little girl. This is a mother who has no time for us and is always tired. And here's the baby who makes her tired with its crying all night long. The spider is Thomas who isn't here and should be.

I let the water catch all the insects in my bath. I drown them all. I watch Martha and the beautiful Rahab who live on the wrong side of the garden whirl down and away in giddy unison.

That night the Dad is playing a Big Band dance record, and while baby Elizabeth sleeps, Mum and he dance on the green silk carpet. The tiredness lifts from my mother's face and she looks happy. Gaga smiles over her knitting and PapaMac drinks his one dram of whisky and peers over the newspaper every now and then. It all seems so normal, just Thomas is missing.

When the news comes on, everyone quietens down. The Dad pulls me onto his lap and strokes my legs through my pyjamas as if everything is going to be all right. As if his forgiveness is mandatory, let alone mine. My mother smiles at me across the room as if all that goes on in the world is pleasant and satisfactory.

As if she sees that he loves me like his own.

VIII

It's our Royal Queen's Birthday Party, Union Jack, brass bands, bagpipes, and biscuits and cake for tea, and a song for our gracious queen even though she won't be there. Mum won't be there either because of the new baby.

Babies aren't much fun, I've decided. They seem to cast a spell on grown-up people that causes them to forget themselves and revert to a language that no one understands. Our baby is tiny and breakable like the bone-china tea set that is brought out only on special occasions and I am not allowed to touch her at all. They have named her Elizabeth like the Queen. Thomas calls her Essie; he says she doesn't look like a queen at all. She's not pretty like Gaga's Jumo. She doesn't have hair and she's wrinkled like an old monkey.

She is only half a sister, Thomas says, because we all have the same mother, but Essie has a different father. When I try to explain this to Martha, she laughs.

'How can you measure love in teaspoons?' she says. 'This is not a recipe... for this one a little more and this a little less. There can be no half-half and step-step. Even your mother's sister is your mother and her child is your sister.'

She scolds Thomas and me for 'cutting our sister in half' for a different father.

'If you love her at all, you must love all of her.'

I wonder if I could ever love the baby as much as my grandmother loves the most precious things in her house, including the treasures in the kist. I am afraid my mother might.

I am holding onto my grandmother's gloved hand. Thomas is here with his class. Almost the whole school is here, rows of St Mark's children clad in the uniform of red, grey and white. On the opposite side of the common the warriors begin to run in and take their places. There are thousands of them, lifting their sticks and spears into the air. A rhythmic voice rises from the earth and the slow beating of shields grows louder, till it drums in your throat like a heartbeat. Then silence.

We face each other across the wide expanse of mowed grass, them and us. The High Commissioner, dressed all in white with a hard hat, stands stiffly beside his wife on a wooden platform that is stage to painted wooden skittle-people, waiting. King Sobhuza, in full tribal splendour, furred and feathered and draped in a dead leopard, sits on a comfortable chair surrounded by a colourful party of royal relations.

Only the Queen, the birthday girl, is missing.

To the left, ranks of uniformed Swazi police stand alongside the Highlanders in tartan skirts behind a brass band that has begun to play the British anthem. The voices around us rise up with patriotic gusto – 'God save our Royal Queen.' Even I know the words – we always stand and sing for our queen before the bioscope at Queensway. Even before Tom and Jerry and Laurel and Hardy. As I join in I feel the pride that swells the chests of all us English, as if we are cheering for the away-team at a cricket match. We sing for another place that we belong to, of a home we've left behind. The half-naked, skin-clad natives before us are utterly still, staring ahead. A few sing along with us, but most just look ahead, impassive.

Then comes the song of *Nkosi Sikelel' iAfrica*, God save Africa, and the ground shakes with the lifting of thousands of voices. This is a hymn, a soulful prayer that thunders across the common and swallows the brass band. Some of the adults around me join in hesitantly. I look across at Thomas. He is singing boldly with some of the others in his class.

After the singing and the speeches, the warriors give a splendid display of primitive dance and war cries that enchant the visitors. The European tourists wait with their cameras, eager to capture this curiosity, this primal stamping of feet in the dust and the raising of shields and spears towards the sky. Isn't the wild life marvellous!

'Woyaah! Wo...wo...wo... Woyaah! Wo!' One voice surging back and rolling forth, swelling upwards, then hushing down to a sibilant whisper, much like the sound of the ocean.

Gaga squeezes my hand tightly in her own as if she thinks I might be carried off by the sound. Or perhaps she is also frightened.

Long trestle tables dressed in starched white tablecloths bow under rows of delicate teacups with silver spoons all facing the same way. For the children, jugs of Oros and paper cups, neat little sandwiches and tiny vanilla cakes that beckon from large silver platters. The warriors disperse, snaking out of the arena like a giant crocodile, slipping away discreetly, back to the valleys and the hills, the mines and the farmlands, and for many, back to the houses and gardens that belong to other people. I suppose there are just too many of them to taste the tea at Queen Elizabeth's tea party.

But that year, 1959, while we sat drinking tea and saluting the absent Queen on her birthday, only a handful of officials knew that negotiations were taking place across the sea that separated us from Europe. King Sobhuza, nodding and smiling above his little grey beard, was more confident than we could guess that English rituals such as this would soon pass away.

IX

It is one night a few days later that the leopard comes back.

I wake to the sound of running, away from the house over the fallen leaves outside the window. The sound of it freezes my limbs, suspends them board-stiff between the sheets. Without Thomas here the leopard has again assumed a threatening significance. I watch the door handle. In my mind I watch her running like a shadow over the flowerbeds, stopping to smell the faint traces of humans in the earth, lifting her eyes towards the house, and the rondavel with the unlocked door. I feel her anticipation in my chest. Martha is breathing heavily under a pile of rugs on her own mattress at the foot of the bed. I crawl down to her and shake her awake.

She stares at me in somnolent confusion as if I don't belong in her dreams.

'She's come back,' I whisper hoarsely.

'No, Miss Jilly. Is nothing. Sleep now.' She forms her words slowly with a tongue still lame with sleep.

The wind has come up and is dragging dried leaves along the cement and stone path.

'The wind is blowing,' she says and turns her head back to her pillow. But I know that scraping sound, and have an inventory in my head of all the other night sounds that Thomas and I listed one by one when we first moved into the rondavel: wind moving leaves, branches creaking, geyser knocking and refilling, eagle owls in the gum trees, the siren that wails a warning in the main house, the sound of native drumming. Thomas and I discovered that when sounds have shapes and names they are no longer as threatening.

'It's not leaves. It's the leopard. It was running outside the window, just like that night Thomas and I saw it.'

'You saw it?'

'Not really saw it, but we heard it. We found its footprints.'

Martha shakes her head and makes a clicking with her tongue.

'Hayi! I don't believe this leopard story.'

'It's true. I promise. Thomas knows all about leopards and Thomas wouldn't lie. He crossed his heart.'

'Maybe Thomas don't lie, but maybe you think something too much and it come true.' Martha begins to rearrange herself on the mattress.

'I want the bathroom light on.'

'Put it on then. But don't come cry tomorrow when the bath she's full of moths.'

I jump from my bed, flick the light switch, and jump back as if the floor itself is crawling.

Then we both hear something above the rustling wind: a sharp bang followed by an inhuman wail, a cry that comes and goes in a split second. Even Martha, half sitting, half lying, stiffens with her ear to the direction of the window.

'The police whistle,' I whisper urgently. 'We have to blow the police whistle.'

'Sssh, Jilly,' she says, and climbs onto my bed with me and wraps me in her arms.

'Tula, lala wena... It not be long till morning.'

But she is wrong. Time stretches on forever when you're waiting. I search my memory for the sound of running I had heard. Did the bang come before the cry or after it? Was there someone out there in the garden? Did the leopard come across that someone and surprise them? What was that other sound? Was it a door banging? Was it a gunshot? Questions wander in circles around my mind and keep sleep from me. From the cradle of Martha's arms I watch the darkness of the night through the curtains till it turns a sweet shade of morning blue.

In the morning a crab spider as big as a saucer lies watching me from the bath while I brush my teeth. He is trapped there. I don't know how he is going to get out, being too big for the plughole – but that is Martha's problem. I am already late for school.

Martha's face is sullen and indifferent as she brings in the tea and eggs for breakfast. She doesn't want to talk about what happened last night. The Ingwe brings trouble, was all she said and No more talk about this!

In the afternoon, I scour the soil for any signs of Shaba, but find none. It is disappointing that everything looks so normal in the light of day; I wish that my brother were here to make what happened last night real.

My mother is in the kitchen spooning KLIM powder into Elizabeth's bottles when I tell her.

'You can sleep in the baby's room if you like, but she cries a lot at night. Just two more nights though and your brother will be home for a long weekend. Can you be brave for two more nights?'

She promises me that a leopard could never open the door, and anyway, she insists, it isn't likely to be a leopard at all, but probably one of the neighbour's dogs out for a midnight stroll.

'And the bang? And the scream?'

'The baby screams at night. Heavens, sometimes she cries for hours. Goodness knows what made the banging noise. I'm sure there's a perfectly reasonable explanation, dear.'

'And the leopard?'

My mother sighs.

'Gillian, please. No more about this.'

I know then that for my mother the leopard isn't real at all.

X

When Thomas comes home he says the jive is out, rock and roll is in, and Elvis is the King. I asked Mum what has happened to our King Sobuhza and Mum and Thomas laugh. Elvis is just the King of Pop she says, not Swaziland.

I can't wait to tell Thomas about the night the leopard came. He is pleased. He says it's time to go up on the hill again and look for spoor. But now he seems more interested in the matinee that's showing in Mbabane, a war film called The Bridge on the River Kwai, with Alec Guinness. All the boys from St Marks are going.

'You can't come, sis,' he said, 'it's too scary for girls. Anyway, you're too young for war flicks.'

But Mum and Martha and I go into town the next day anyway. My mother lets me walk around the market with Martha in tow while she stops in almost every shop to order this and that to be delivered, our meat, dogs' meat, servants' meat from the butcher, skeins of bright fabric for sewing, sugar and flour and a range of boxes and packets from Mohammed's General Store. The market smells of sisal mats and baskets, baboon-tail grass and pineapple. There are Tamboti wood bowls, impala skins, buffalo tails, seed beads, glass beads, and lucky bean necklace strings, and there on the ground on bright fabric cloths, green paw-paw and banana bunches, sweet pink guavas, oranges and naartjies and avocado pears.

I want a miniature cowhide shield complete with stick knobkerrie and tin spear. Martha thrusts a piece of sugar cane in my hand instead. When it begins to rain, she opens her black umbrella, hoists up her skirts, and we both run up the road to take shelter outside the fish and chips shop, taking comfort in the warm vinegar and hot potato smells that waft out the door. Then we shuffle to the chemist's, bound together by a shared umbrella, for Eno's fruit salts for Rahab's tummy ache. Mum is browsing in Gresham's for a new dress.

In the post office my mother collects our letters and Gaga's *Women's Weekly* from overseas. I wave and grin at Martha who stands in the native section on the other side, buying stamps for her letters to Zululand.

I hope we can stop at the tearoom for a strawberry milk shake, but Martha can't sit with us my mother says, and it is too wet and miserable for her to wait outside. I whine and sulk all the way home. Why can't I have a Swazi cowhide shield? Why must Martha stay outside in the rain? Why?

Both Martha and my mother look at the road ahead and say nothing. The sound of the wipers dragging on the windscreen punctuates the strained silence that grows between them. And I whine on like the rain.

My mother slams her hands down on the steering wheel.

'Just because, Gillian. It's the way it is. That's all. Now keep quiet or I'll drop you off at the side of the road and you can walk home in the rain!'

XI

Thomas has found fresh animal tracks around the chicken coop, but they don't belong to Shaba. He thinks they might belong to a jackal and tells the Dad.

'No doubt about it,' the Dad says. 'It was trying to steal the chickens.'

Solomon must secure the wire netting around the coop, and the chickens are settled in behind the wire mesh in the evening. The Dad takes out his guns and cleans them with Thomas's help.

'Are we going to shoot it?' he asks.

'If we have to.'

Thomas is captivated by the thought of stalking jackals with a real gun and he asks the Dad when he is going to teach him to shoot.

'We'll go down to Malkerns to the canning factory tomorrow, if the rain stops. There's a vacant lot of land at the back. I'll put up some targets.'

That night Thomas keeps me awake with his talk of hunting and shotguns. He just won't stop, until I ask him:

'What'll happen if they find Shaba's footprints in the garden? Will Dad find her and shoot her?'

Thomas lies there thinking for a while.

'We shouldn't tell them anything about the leopard. They don't believe it anyway, but just in case...'

We are both lying in our beds looking up at the thatch. The rain is pouring down outside and I wonder how the grass could keep out so much water. Thomas is quiet now.

'Did you see Rahab up at the compound?'

'What's that?' Thomas asks.

'Not that – who. Rahab is Martha's daughter. She's just like a princess.'

'I dunno. I didn't see anyone up at the compound – just Solomon and Moses. I wish with all my might this rain would stop. Please God, let it stop.'

By late morning it has stopped though the clouds are still eiderdown-thick and folded over the valley, and the mountains have vanished. Thomas and the Dad load the guns into the car while Mum and I watch them from the lounge window.

'God, how I hate guns,' my mother says as she watches them drive away.

'I hate the canning factory anyway,' I say, a vague disappointment rising in my throat, thinking how it might be better to have been born a boy. It is true about the factory, though. It's a huge concrete space with teeth-rattling machines, the sickly sweet smell of pineapples, and dark wells of hydrochloric acid that can eat your flesh in minutes. There'd be nothing left of you except maybe your shoe buckles. Keep away from the grinding wheels and oiled black machine teeth that will grab you sleeve-first and spit chopped wedges of you out onto a conveyor belt like tinned People Fruit.

On a rare visit there, I hug my waist, shoes welded to cold concrete, afraid to move, in case only my shoe buckles or a tin of me is left for my mother to cry over when the rest of me was gone.

The Dad makes us tea in his office. Behind his door he keeps a sjambok, a long black whip made of leather with a stout plaited leather handle. He laughs when he tells us it is for whipping small children and the natives in the factory who are lazy or troublesome. Thomas and I smile shyly, but we aren't sure that it isn't true. Why else does he keep it hidden behind his office door?

XII

The beautiful Rahab has left for Durban in Moses' second-hand car. She held both of my hands and spoke softly in Zulu and although I didn't understand the words, I knew that she liked me and would miss me. Martha was swollen with tears as Moses pulled out on the gravel drive in his new second-hand car. We watched the car disappear in the dust through the white brick gates and away.

'She'll be back. Not too long from now. She getting married.' Martha blew her nose into a huge white hankie, damp with tears. Rahab was to marry the first son of a chief from the Eshowe district, to be his first wife.

'He's still young,' Martha said wistfully.

'Will you go to the wedding?' I asked.

'I'm going, yes. Big huge wedding, lasting so – two whole days. They kill the cows and make very huge party.' She looked over my head into a distance that went beyond the mountains. She had never spoken about the day we shelled peas together, and I never said a word about what the Dad had said. But she did confide in me that she was not sorry that Moses had left.

'He is like the foot of the baboon,' she said and, seeing my puzzled look, added: 'He bring too much trouble from the city. Better not to talk trouble.'

I didn't know what this trouble was and Martha showed no inclination to tell me. Anyway, Gaga always said that Native Trouble was none of our business.

Rahab would be married at the groom's kraal, before a huge gathering of people. They would come across the valleys and hills of Zululand bearing gifts and tokens from live chickens to little trinkets from local trading stores.

A big lobolo would be paid for Rahab, more than six head of cattle, and her family would raise a white flag high up on a pole outside their beehive hut, as a witness to the coming marriage. Martha and the other wives of the Induna would dress Rahab with careful attention to detail. They would tie white cow-tail fringes on her upper arms and below her knees. On her wrist she would wear the gall bladder of a goat slaughtered by her father the day before. Her necklace would be a wide collar of beadwork, mainly in white for purity, with long strands of beads that hang between her breasts.

Rahab would curtsy before her groom, her eyes caste down, and present him with the sharply honed blade of a shaftless spear, giving him her virginity. He would take the spear blade from her as a gift, and then lead the dance, spinning and lunging suggestively towards her, with moans and deep-throated cries from the other men, who move forwards and back in a mesmerizing wave.

The dancing will become passionate and frenzied and, along with the intoxication of home-brewed beer, will arouse in the groom a fervour that only his wife can quench. He will raise his hand and the crowd will quietly disappear like a retreating tide, and he will take his wife into his kraal.

PART THREE

Joseph's story

There was a fresh kill last night.

Winston and the others have been following the leopard for seven weeks now, even at night, but have only once witnessed an actual kill. This morning the corpse of a zebra foal hung from the branches of a thorn tree just outside the Ironwood forest. The thorns are long and sharp and white like a cage of prehistoric teeth. The striped fur is still soft and long; still a suckling. Its velvet muzzle is split by an uneven grin.

The leopard was not with the kill though, so we moved into the forest quietly. She sat high up on her usual perch, and from under her thick paws leered another corpse. This time a warthog, a medium-sized female but a heavy weight to haul halfway up a tree.

She has taken advantage of the vulnerable. My guess is that she hunted the warthog first, driven by hunger, because this prey is widely available but does not give in without ferocious argument. The foal, the newborn, would have been an easy target, a sweet bonus.

This wilderness is never without threat and it is some consolation knowing that Joseph Maseko, our steadfast Swazi tracker, is armed with more than a camera and knows this terrain well. He grew up in the valley near Mbabane, so we share a kinship. Perhaps he even ran with the young men, carrying luseki branches for King Sobhuza for Incwala. I wonder if that khaki hides a true warrior.

The other Swazi trackers, George and Abraham, speak little English but excel at setting up camp, and they carry Winston's load of equipment with ease over the rocky terrain bristling with needle-sharp grass stubble. They are usually without shoes, the soles of their feet toughened and worn.

Joseph Maseko is unusually talkative at camp this afternoon. He loves a good story and this one is interspersed with guffaws of unrestrained laughter. It goes something like this:

It was a fine day in Mpumalanga when a white farmer, strolling the boundaries of his land, came across twelve sheep hanging in the branches above him. Needless to say he was astonished and dismayed because they happened to be his own. When he eventually found the herd boy he gave him a sound hiding first and then asked him how all his sheep had landed up in the tree, every one stone dead.

Through his inconsolable sobbing the boy told the farmer his sorry tale.

He was squatting on his haunches, his herding stick propped up, minding the sheep at a good patch of grass when he caught sight of a leopard moving stealthily towards his charges. He ran away as fast as he could and hid behind a distant boulder, leaving the sheep stupidly huddled in one spot, easy prey for the leopard. The boy watched from his hiding place as the leopard took them one by one into the trees. Only two of the sheep were gutted; the others lay untouched except for the single bite to the spine that had efficiently broken their necks. Stiff-legged woolsacks perched in the branches – a macabre sight indeed for anyone to stumble across.

With the telling of the tale the night air has grown chilly. The clouds have settled, obliterating the surrounding mountains. Even our tents have vanished from sight. The mist has wrapped our huddled group in eerie isolation, reflecting a red tinge where it meets the fire's smoke. We are in the spotlight, like performers on a stage, the script in the hands of the storytellers.

Someone says that leopards will take dogs. They'll leave the humans to sleep and drag the dogs from under the beds.

Winston rakes the coals and adds another log.

'A leopard can lure a dog from the safety of a back door,' he says, 'or tease it with guttural cat sounds, rustling the bushes on the edge of a garden. It's simply her cunning and persistence.'

'Would a leopard take a human child? I mean, if the opportunity…'

'She'll steal a baby off a mother's back, and such stories are not uncommon. There have been cases in India where more than a hundred villagers have been carried away by a single leopard over a period of less than a year.'

'And in Africa?'

'There are tribes that place their corpses or even the dying out in the forests or in the open bushveld, exposed to hyenas and vultures. They are said to carry away the spirits of the dead. But it's a problem even today. The leopard feeds on the cadavers and gets a taste for human flesh, especially after an epidemic when bodies are plentiful and the leopard finds itself with an easy dinner every night.

'When the corpses run out it moves to the edge of the villages at night and snatches live humans to satisfy its now acquired taste for human flesh.'

I feel a wave of exhaustion overcoming my enthusiasm. I have accumulated enough macabre imagery to feed the nightmares I'm sure await me in my tent.

II

Last night, Joseph told us another story. He had moved towards the fire, sitting as close to us as was respectful, belonging as he does to a generation of people accustomed to certain mores. Winston threw a couple of logs on the smouldering coals and the flames licked up again, swirling the ember-flecked smoke upwards to dissolve in the mist.

Joseph Maseko is not as old as he looks. The deep lines etched into his face are deceptive; he is not much older than myself. By the light of the fire his face glowed unnaturally red against the night's shadows. He seems to have spent a lifetime collecting stories and anecdotes, most of them first-hand accounts, others passed on by word of mouth in the age-old tradition of Africa. As he spoke, he looked into the fire, his bright eyes appearing to reach beyond what they saw into that distant place where the storyteller keeps his sources.

'It is the story of my uncle who has known this thing of the bantwana taken in the night by the leopard. This happen long time past – can be –'58 or maybe '59. Me, I am a young boy not yet a man – twelve years or whatever. My uncle, he is Petrus – very old man now. He is staying that time on Pili-kins farm past Mbabane. It is in the afternoon when they come to call him, the other white baas and a native boy from the other place, other side Pili-kins farm. They call Petrus because he be good tracker like me.'

He smiled broadly at this and looked up at our faces for approval.

'He'm good with the shotgun, see. Big Baas Pili-kins show him good how to shoot. They go up-up in North Africa many times to shoot the what-what for the biltong, make skins sometime for Missus Pili-kins. But this time he must come carry the shotgun for to kill the leopard.

'Why the leopard? he is asking.

'No, this leopard is the one who takes the small one in the middle of the night. That is what they tell him.'

Joseph continued casting his broken English into the mountain mist like an invisible net, forming and expanding images in our minds, master weaver of the tale.

It was early evening when they eventually set out. It was unwise to start the hunt so late. A leopard has full advantage at night, especially when there is cloud cover. The two white men had argued about this. Pilkins insisted it was sheer madness, better to leave it till morning, and besides she could be moving about anywhere in those hills and mountains; it could take days to track her down.

But the other white man was unyielding. She would be on the prowl at night, by day she might hide anywhere high up on the hill or in a cave along the precipice of the mountain gorge. He would have her that night, he insisted.

Along the side of the hill the earth was still scorched by a fire that had swept through the valley from the pine plantation. The hunters moved over the blackened earth with difficulty; in the fading light of evening there was little distinction between the dead stony ground and the charred stumps of trees and shrubs. There were two white men with guns and three trackers. Of the black men, only Petrus carried a weapon.

They moved slowly and silently up the dark hillside, careful not to raise the ash dust with their boots, choosing each step with care. When they reached the summit of the hill, they divided into two groups. Petrus and the other white man continued down the gorge towards the mountain and Pilkins and the rest made for the far side of the hill where the fire had stopped. The bush was thick with wattle and thorn trees and the veld grass as high as a man's waist.

It was a misty evening, and cloudy, and though the moon was bright, it was veiled and gave little light. By the time Petrus and his companion reached the foot of the mountain it was so dark on the ground they could barely see their own feet outside of the torchlight. They felt their way up the rocky side of the mountain, stopping now and then to listen to the silence. The mists began to fold over the mountain top and move down towards them.

'Better to go back,' Petrus whispered.

A night like this was the perfect cover for a leopard to creep silently behind them unnoticed. But nothing could stop the other man. It was as if he knew she would be there.

As they stood there, looking back towards the scattered lights of the farmhouses, they heard a baboon call out, followed by the answering cries of her young. They stood still in the silence that followed, listening.

That was when they heard the plaintive call of a leopard. Petrus had heard that call before, the call of the mother cat for her young. She was unaware as yet of her pursuers, so they still had the advantage. He wanted to whisper to the white man that there might be babies and the leopardess would be dangerous, sure to attack them to protect her young. But he was afraid of the sound of his own voice; he did not know how close she was.

In the enclosing mist sounds echoed and shifted direction, causing the two men to hesitate, unsure of which way to proceed. They must have waited more than an hour, the damp beginning to soak through their clothes. Petrus wondered if he should quietly retreat and leave the white man here with his own madness. But a black man had no business running away from the courage of the white hunter, however foolish. He knew that more certainly than he feared for his life.

'That white baas was hungry for the blood of the leopard. Petrus, he can feel the anger, here in the white man's heart. He stop every time to drink from the bottle he keeps in his pocket, he hold the gun up every time he hear something on the mountain. They move slowly-

slowly in the dark. Now Petrus, he is wet and cold, so he don't hold the gun straight. He think that if the leopard see him first, he die one time. No second chance.'

In the light of the torch a cluster of granite boulders loomed up ahead. The white man handed his torch to Petrus, who directed the beam over the surface of the rock and up towards the top.

The rest happened too quickly to remember clearly. Petrus thought he saw the torchlight reflected in the cat's eyes above them and he swung round, losing his footing and stumbling in the dark. That was when the torch fell. He heard the sharp crack of the rifle as the long dark shadow of the leopard flew over him, then the sound of the beast and the man tumbling down over the rocks below. Then everything was quiet again.

Shivering with the shock or the cold, he could not tell which, Petrus did not dare call out in case the leopard was still alive, crouching on the rocks below, waiting for him. He sat on his haunches, his gun poised at the ready, but he wondered if he was not too weak, too afraid to put up much of a fight. He stared into the darkness like a blind man waiting to die.

Then he heard a whistle from just below his feet, clear across the night, followed by a shout for help, and he knew that the big cat was dead. Petrus could smell the blood on the white man as he struggled to pull him up over the ledge. He must have lain under the leopard for a full five minutes. He was soaked in blood from his head to his boots.

The man had stood there breathless, cursing and laughing at the same time, trembling, thrilled with the kill.

'Fucking lucky shot! God's truth, a fucking bloody miracle!'

They stumbled back along the ridge in the dark. The white man threw his head back every now and then and laughed at the sky. By the time they met up with the others it was almost midnight and the clouds had dispersed enough to let the moon peer down on the five men walking home.

'In the morning they go back for the leopard and carry it back to the house, other side Pili-kin's farm, to show them that this one that comes to take their children is truly dead.'

We sat and watched the last embers of the fire smoulder. It was a good story, well told, a satisfying tale to end the day. Though of course Maggie, Winston's wife, wanted to know more. She had to concern herself with the details. When did they know that the leopard killed the child? Did they find the body? Whose child was it?

Joseph shook his head and shrugged. It was not his story, he said, so that was all he knew. He pulled his grey blanket about himself and moved back into the shadows to sleep between the folded canvas tarpaulin in the hollow beneath the tree with the other trackers.

I sat there watching the fire grow cold and ash white, feeling as though I was stepping onto unknown ground, uncertainly.

I crawled back into the tent just before midnight, exhausted but unable to sleep. I have come so far now, but it seems the more that is uncovered the more I want to shrink back into the safe shelter of forgetting, the amnesic numbness that is so much easier to live with.

When I was twenty years old, I woke up one morning to the startling realization that innocence had left me. It had been taken from me inch by inch unnoticed for years. The epiphany came in a moment and left me feeling strangely bereft.

After listening to Joseph Maseko's story, I felt the same sense of rushing towards the inevitable, too late to turn back.

III

The valley sings in a frenzy of expectation. It is late July 1959 and the season of the Reed Dance.

This is the time for Swazi maidens to present themselves to the king, to dance shyly before their prospective grooms, to collect river reeds for the queen mother's kraal. Anticipation flutters through the kingdom as girls prepare themselves for womanhood, preening, vaselining, and arranging their costumes for the dance. They will walk for miles, winding over hills and through valleys, joining together in celebration of womanhood, a veritable virginal crocodile.

For us the long holidays are filled with our own expectations. Our Uncle Hugh will be coming to stay for at least a week and Thomas can hardly contain his delight. The Dad has bought my brother a Daisy pellet gun and is going to take him back to Malkerns for an afternoon of target practice.

The era of rock and roll has filtered down to even the remotest parts of Africa. All the kids are talking about Elvis and Thomas is swept up with this new mania. He has bought a single playing record of 'Wooden Heart' and plays it endlessly on Papa's record player. We both know all the words and sing them endlessly throughout the holidays. The leopard scrapbook lies unfinished and forgotten for a while in the top drawer of the cupboard.

PapaMac and Gaga are going to Jo'burg in the Pontiac at the start of the holidays. For a whole week we are to practise being a real family. Without the restraint of parents-in-law, the Dad slips comfortably into his new role as head of the household. He assumes full control of the kitchen, revealing the depths of his epicurean nature.

First of all, he introduces us to 'braaivleis-'n-putu', raw meat and boerewors, charred on an open fire, and stiff maize porridge. This is when he throws Thomas his first culinary challenge – the eating of raw wors. When my brother squirms at the idea, the Dad says:

'For Pete's sake, Thomas, you're such a girl. Wouldn't harm you to get that hair cut either. When's the beauty contest?'

I watch Thomas swallow the raw pink flesh, his eyes staring into the fire. You can tell he is desperate to please the Dad. I would never go that far, but then, I am a girl.

'You see? An African hunter who can master a rifle shouldn't balk at the idea of a little raw meat.'

But that is only the beginning. His plan is to animalise my brother into the brotherhood of sanguinary appetites, the next initiation into men's business.

Thomas takes the bait to save face, but by the end of the week I am a confirmed vegetarian.

One day I come into the kitchen and find the pink and naked body of a suckling pig lying belly up on the kitchen counter. It lies there, forearms folded in supplication, its snout wrinkled above a pouting mouth and its lashed eyelids closed to its fate. The piglet is perfectly sweet and even though it is also perfectly dead, I do not seem able to recognize the fact. I cannot comprehend death in something so dear. I have not yet seen the death of anything bigger than the insects I regularly drown in the bath.

I stroke its upturned belly, and feel the folds beneath my fingers. It is not unlike streaking Baby Essie's smooth tummy with Johnson's baby powder. So when the Dad takes out the herbs, salt and oil and bastes it for the oven, I am horror struck at what awaits it.

'This will be a dinner you'll never forget!' he announces.

He is right about never forgetting.

The baby piglet is dressed in rosemary and garlic with half an apple in its mouth – he couldn't fit a whole one in. It is presented to us whole and complete at the dinner table. I stare in mesmerized disbelief, and so does Thomas. The Dad is telling my Mum a story of a native waiter who, when asked to dress a wild pig for dinner and to make sure that the apple was in the pig's mouth, came into the dining hall with the roasted carcass covered in a white table cloth. And the apple?

'Well of course, the apple was in the mouth of the well-intentioned kaffir, wasn't it?'

Thomas joins in the laughter. He is trying so hard. I can't stop staring at the crisped snout with the upturned nostrils.

'I don't want to eat the baby pig,' I say.

'You will eat it. I spent the whole bloody afternoon in the kitchen,' says the Dad, his good humour suddenly spent.

'You can't make me.'

'Gillian,' my mother interjects nervously.

'It's only a baby. How can you kill a baby and then eat it?'

The Dad plunges the carving knife into the soft place behind the folded ear.

'I won't have you sticking your nose up at good food. Pass me your plate.'

'Gillian!'

'Gillian!'

I have picked up my plate and deliberately turned it upside-down. I push back my chair and rush from the dining table. My mother apologises for the bad manners of another man's daughter.

I am in a state of disgrace for the rest of the week. In the Dad's book, disgrace means being completely ignored, as if you aren't there.

It suits me well; my antipathy for the Dad and for eating the flesh of living things have been growing in equal measure. I will eat only the white starch on my plate, refusing anything with colour, even gravy. Mum is afraid I'll die of malnutrition. The Dad says he's never heard of a white person dying of malnutrition — she will start eating again when she's hungry — she should think herself lucky not to be starving like the millions of poor people in the world who can't afford to eat.

Thomas has bravely, though reluctantly, bitten the bacon to prove that he can match the Dad's challenge, to stop the taunting. It's just another game that men and boys play, and they never tire of it.

By the end of the week the Dad has exhausted the variety of bloody feasts, all guaranteed to provoke a squeamish response. The best way to present a fish is with the head on, the eyes being a delicacy in some countries. He picks them out delicately with forefinger and thumb and swallows them whole. The Dad says that the finest lamb roast is judged by the amount of blood that spills into the dish as you cut the first slice. He might be right, in culinary terms. It is the way he sets about it that is offensive. He holds out a spoon of warm blood and offers it first to me and then to Thomas. Thomas feigns satisfaction and hides his grimace behind his serviette. I stare fixedly at the blandness on my plate.

Boiled potato and rice, salted, colourless, plain. The Holy Sacraments that Martha speaks of take on a grim significance. No one will ever persuade me to drink blood, even if it means an eternity in hell. My mother, meanwhile, is taking mental notes of the Dad's likes and dislikes to cater for future meals.

Oh, is that how you like it? I must remember to do it in that particular way.

I ask myself how long a person can survive only on bread and jam and roast potatoes. When Thomas and I are alone I burst out:

'Killing animals is cruel. I'll never eat meat again.'

'Aw, it's just like killing insects and we kill them all the time,' says Thomas.

'That's different.'

"Snot."

"Tis so, cause when you drown them there's no blood and we don't eat insects.'

'Dad eats live mopani worms.'

'Sis, man, that's disgusting. Like eating live silkworms.'

Thomas says that the Dad got used to eating raw meat and things like suckling pigs when he was living as a hunter in the bush. It's something men get used to when there aren't any women around.

'He's even eaten snakes and crocodiles and sheep's brains cooked in their heads,' says Thomas.

'He better not make us eat those. If he does, I'm running away!'

Thomas shrieks with laughter.

I fold my arms, bitterly hating everything to do with Men's Business.

The Dad says this is how it will be when it's just the five of us, living in our own house when we move to Rhodesia. We'll get a dog and a cat and live like a normal family. I think everything has been normal enough up till now, but Thomas is pleased. The Dad says he can't wait to take my brother out into the real bush and hunt springbok and impala and make biltong. He explains the whole procedure, from skinning and gutting the buck and cutting the meat into long thin strips, rubbing it with coarse salt and spices and hanging the meat for weeks in the garage under a warm tin roof.

'We'll go up to the Zambezi dam, and take a boat into the middle, where the water is as warm as your bath. There are baobab trees to climb, the biggest trees you've ever seen, that look as if they've been planted upside-down,' he says.

'In the evenings, we'll sit outside and watch the sun go down as late as nine o' clock and the grown-ups will drink sundowners on the veranda and the children will run on the lawns and play in their pyjamas.'

My mother sits with Baby Essie on her lap and smiles at Thomas and me, tilting her head slightly, a fond inclination that says: This is what I've always wanted for all of us.

My imagination cannot take me further than the reaches of our garden and the valleys and hills of Swaziland. Rhodesia is a place that is so far away, so far out of reach. How can one comprehend a world divorced from Gaga and Papa and Martha?

IV

Lally sits on a wicker chair, her long legs swinging from a layered bell of petticoats and a wide skirt. She keeps throwing her hair back and sighing audibly as if she is sending telepathic messages over our heads, invisible letters in invisible ink, addressed to Heavens Above.

Apart from the braces on her teeth that make her speak slowly and carefully as if her mouth is full of peanut butter, our cousin has grown secretive. She disappears into the insect bathroom for hours and comes out looking just the same, though she holds her head differently, in an awkward tilt, as if it might fall from her shoulders while someone is looking. When you speak to her she looks past you at the windows that look back at her. Our mother says it's because she is growing up.

A couple of days after Lally, our uncle Hugh arrives from Johannesburg with a Meccano set, complete with levers and pulleys, screws and bolts and brightly coloured metal plates. Our Uncle Hugh is the sort of person everyone wants to be with. He always comes bearing gifts.

Gaga says he is her gift, her *laat lammetjie*.

'My lamb,' she says, 'you've grown so tall.'

'You've grown short, Ma,' he says, bending low to kiss her cheek.

He is the only one who dares to tease my grandmother.

That night the Lamb takes centre stage in our rondavel. We are sitting on our beds in our pyjamas. Uncle Hugh sits on the wicker chair framed by the window and the navy blue sky.

'A leopard comes into our garden at night.'

'A leopard you say? Hmmm. And you've seen it?'

'Thomas has seen it,' I say.

'I heard her outside the window.'

'Hmmm.' He nods slowly. 'Did you really see something, Thomas? Something that looked like a leopard, or did you just hear it?'

Thomas retrieves his scrapbook from his drawer.

Uncle Hugh reads the notes, his eyes scanning the pages rapidly under a serious frown. Then he comes across the tracings of the paw prints, the two that belonged to Shaba and the jackal one.

'Where did you trace these from, Tommy? From a book?'

'No.'

'He traced them from the ground, outside the window,' I say.

'Promise?'

'Word of honour,' says Thomas, slapping his hand across his chest.

We all start talking at once, and Uncle Hugh raises his hand.

'Ssssh! Let me see if I can remember this.'

He stands to attention. In the lamplight he looks as if he is famous, as if he belongs on the screen of the Queen's Way bioscope. His hair is brushed back smooth and dark, except for a stray lick that keeps falling over his forehead. His voice is deep and rich with intonation, the sort of voice that makes you feel safe and sure, like the colour of the plum velvet curtains in Gaga's lounge.

'When the moon gets up and the night comes,
He is the cat that walks by himself, and all places are alike to him.
Then he goes out to the Wet... Wild...Woods... or
Up the Wet... Wild... Trees... waving his
Wild tail and walking... by his wild lone.'

He gives an exaggerated bow and the three of us clap and cheer, fiercely adoring his every word.

'It's from a poem by Rudyard Kipling. Now if you're all good for the next few days, we might just go for a walk along the Usutu and visit Mantenga Falls for a picnic. Then we'll talk more about this leopard of yours.'

He winks at Thomas.

'I think the name you've chosen for her is grand.'

True to his word, Uncle Hugh coaxes a fine picnic out of Gaga's kitchen: cake, cold roast chicken sandwiches for the others and cheese for me. The picnic is on the day before the Reed Dance, a ceremony that we are forbidden to watch. Too many half-naked savages and hundreds of bare breasts for all the world to see, says Gaga. But Uncle Hugh is going with his camera and promises us a secret viewing of the photographs afterwards.

It's a long walk along a stony orange path that cuts into the thick forest, rustling with countless birds and small creatures. As the path meanders down to the river we come across a noisy fellowship of green pigeons breakfasting high up in the branches of a waterberry tree, a haphazard arrangement of startling bright feathers. They adopt strange acrobatic postures to reach the black fruit, every loud screech a territorial protest.

The edge of the Usutu River is thick with tall reeds, white thorn acacias, Sicalaba, Tamboti, thick wattle and weeping ferns and, on the ground, scattered buck droppings like piles of pebbles. All around us mountains rise up, gold with grass below sheer granite; we are like four ants in this green valley bowl. High above, eyes follow us from between the giant grey slabs and sleeping boulders. This is leopard country. Caracal, baboon, duiker, reedbuck and klipspringer dwell here.

High above, Nyonyane Peak watches over the valley. Execution Rock lies here – for thieves, murderers and wayward subjects of the king. With a spear at your back and an unforgiving drop below, this is the point of no return. No one can remember, though, when last a body fell from this terrible height.

Along the river's edge the smell of wet stones is raw and fresh. We walk barefoot across the smooth black rocks where we can. The water is clear and icy cold, even though the late winter sun is generous. Uncle Hugh insists that we each carry a stick. In the heart of Mantenga, surrounding the falls, there are snakes and leguaans. We tap the rocks as we walk to announce our presence.

We've laid out our picnic on a wide slab of rock and we are watching the twin falls from a safe distance, though you can still feel the soft spray on your face when the wind turns. Above the waterfalls the hills are lush with giant gum trees, green and lovely. A variety of birds swoop down the rock face and flit in and out of the rising smoke that drifts up from the roiling water below. Uncle Hugh's head is a dictionary of names we've never heard. Lilac-breasted Rollers, Plum-coloured Starlings, Woodland Kingfishers, Red-backed Shrikes.

With our eyes closed we can hear better, the rushing waterfalls, the creaking of Kiaat and Tamboti branches, the breeze in the Sicalaba and the Tassel Berry, the rise and fall of vervet monkey chatter in the high canopies in the distance. Out of the medley of sound come the voices of young girls.

We open our eyes, startled.

They flutter out of the trees a few yards from us like butterflies. They have seen the four of us sitting there, but ignore us and begin to undress. They don't seem to mind an audience.

These young Swazi maidens have come down to the river to wash themselves for tomorrow's Reed Dance. It is customary, our uncle says.

Thomas wears a wide embarrassed smile, but never closes his eyes once. Lally tosses her head and rolls her eyes. 'Oh God, how embarrassing, I can't bear it!'

'It's all perfectly natural. Beautiful young girls washing in an open-air bathroom, getting ready for a dance. Imagine if all this was your bathroom, Lally?'

Lally blushes and folds her arms, turning her back on the maidens.

'And now they will each cut a handful of tall river reeds for the queen mother, and tomorrow they will dress in tassles and beads, with the tail feathers of birds in their soft black hair. Any one of them might be chosen as a wife tomorrow. Maybe even the new wife of old King Sobhuza.'

Lally covers her face with her hands and groans.

'Oh God, I can't...'

Don't say any more and spoil this day. I leap up and begin jumping over the rocks back up the river towards the way we came. Jumping rocks is a knack and, compared with Thomas and Lally, I am easily the most skilled, never slipping, never missing the mark once, a true klipspringer. Aim with your eyes first and send your mind ahead.

I stop to let the others catch up, not inclined to risk a quarrel with a leguaan on my own.

'Hey, Jilly!'

Uncle Hugh is holding a long scarlet feather.

'Do you know what the bird is?'

I take it from him. It's perfect, undamaged. I hold it in the palm of my hand.

'What bird is it?'

'The Purple-crested Loerie, royal bird of kings and princesses. You'd better hide it away.'

'Why must I?'

'Because, darling, you might be my little princess, but you're not a Swazi princess. Only royal princesses are allowed to wear red loerie feathers!'

I hold it up to the sunlight. It's true scarlet, the colour of royal blood. There are moments when an object as small and light as a feather can change one's whole perspective. If I were born a princess, I now know for certain, it would be a whole lot better to be a princess of the royal Swazi king than to be Princess Anne. I promise to hide it away as soon as we get home. Under the stones of my own special place, it'll bring a touch of royal magic.

Uncle Hugh takes my hand in his. It slows down the rock jumping as he's more careful and deliberate with the placing of his feet, but there is great comfort in the size and firmness of his hand. I try to think of something important to say. I remember the leopard.

'Uncle Hugh, would Shaba ever hurt us? She wouldn't come into our garden in the daytime, would she?'

His reply is comforting.

'She's a night time hunter, really. It's quite possible she came down to survey the possibility of nabbing her dinner from the chicken coop. Leopards aren't usually interested in humans. Don't you go worrying your little head about it.'

V

Perhaps Uncle Hugh is more worried about the leopard than he seemed. He asks the Dad that night about the guns. The Dad's as pleased as a John Wayne. They leave the table and go through to the lounge where the Dad keeps his guns in the long Imbuia cupboard that's padlocked. They speak in grey gravel tones, the seriousness of men and weapons, and I can see that Thomas is straining to hear. He is eating slowly, so that the grown-ups won't send us off to bed yet.

We hear the Dad laugh out loudly.

'... and the only good kaffir is a dead one!'

My mother sits up stiff in her chair and presses her serviette to her mouth.

Utter silence stops spoons mid-air on their way to open mouths.

Uncle Hugh's voice is clear and calm:

'I can't say I appreciate that kind of attitude.'

The Dad mumbles something offstage.

The reply rises steadily in a wave of irritation.

It evokes a stream of words from the Dad, spoken in full-throated anger

'... your type with those big bloody words... university... the reality of... a kaffir who knows he's a kaffir is the only black man worth his salt!'

The sound of ice against glass, glass against glass.

'Where the hell did my sister find the likes of you?'

My mother's mouth is still covered with a serviette and her eyes brim with real tears. She pushes back her chair and hurries from the dining room towards the passage.

PapaMac stands up and walks slowly into the lounge, weary parent assessing war damage. Gaga looks pale and her mouth has that bird-beak look, pinched tight with displeasure.

'Hurry up and finish your dinner,' she barks in a loud whisper and she gives the bell a quick flick of her wrist. With the dependable timing of a cuckoo clock, Patience comes through the kitchen door.

'No, go back!' Gaga snaps. 'I'll call you. Go back.' Patience curtsies and walks backwards through the door again.

'Gillian, for goodness sakes, get yourself up and go to your room,' my grandmother says.

I ease myself off the chair and idle towards the door.

'Thomas and Alice, you too. Hurry up!' Gaga hovers over the table, flapping her wrists at us. Then she turns and goes straight through the kitchen door herself, leaving us all standing in the dining room looking down at the table of porcelain plates and half-finished puddings.

We hear Papa's voice smooth and calm, pouring his moderate sensibilities over the confrontation. But Hugh's voice rises above it again.

'What the hell world do you think you're living in? Do you think… living in this little kingdom… protect… happening in the rest of Africa? Do you … the brutality and torture…?'

The Dad's voice:

'We have to keep them in their place or they'll all turn to violence. Look at Kenya!'

Now they are all shouting, and the three of us are still standing in a huddle near the door rooted stiff-legged to the floor, waiting for the sound of gunshot.

'You put them all in the same basket – just a bunch of primitives, even Ma sees them that way. She's bloody terrified they'll turn on us and murder us in our beds!'

The Dad again:

'You just can't put us all together in one big pot. It'll never work…'

'If they rise up with one voice…'
'… our cultures are too different.'
'They have risen up with one voice already, Pops.'
'… if they are not separated…'
'They are simply driving the ANC underground.'
'You liberals are all the bloody same.'
'… every one of us could be in danger.'
'Can you imagine one of our daughters stuck up against a wall with one of them?'

There's a long pause.

Them is a shadow word for nameless and dangerous others.

For now the reasoning behind all this adult anger is lost on us, but we will grow up learning these phrases that are to echo many times over other dinners and over cigarettes and drinks, sipped and savoured in other places. For now it isn't what Uncle Hugh is saying as much as the fact that no one else wants to listen. Who is right and who is wrong in this argument? In the end I know only that poor Thomas's loyalties are cut in the middle between the two men he most wants to believe in.

Hugh's voice has grown coldly calm.

'This is the beginning of the end of the privileged white life, of eating cake and throwing crumbs to the grateful blacks.'

'Kaffir-boetie talk! They'll sooner stab you in your back for your hypocritical consideration… Christ!'

The Dad sweeps through the hall and straight out through the front door, slamming it shut behind him.

The three of us are suddenly stumbling over each other in our haste to reach the passage and the safety of the rondavel.

No words pass between us when we climb into our beds that night. Thomas has his face buried in his pillow.

I lie there in the dark, in the aftershock, looking up at lizard-land and praying for Normal to return in the morning. Can't understand grown-up talk. Everyone blames everyone, for being angry, for being afraid. Something dangerous is going to happen. And if they're so frightened... I have never seen my mother cry before. Are mothers supposed to cry? The Dad said kaffir. There is no doubt that our Uncle Hugh is angry with the Dad. Somehow that thought pleases me.

Tomorrow I will go to Martha. She is always the same. She is strong and wise and never afraid of anything.

As I am sinking into the oblivion of sleep, I hear Lally whisper into the darkness.

'Do you think they'll really murder us in our beds?'

There is no reply. What answer could there be to such a question?

VI

In the morning our Uncle Hugh has left. We dare to anticipate his return after the Reed Dance later that day, but he doesn't come back.

Gaga says, 'Gone back to Jo'burg. Grown-ups Business.'

My mother lies on her bed with one of her headaches that leave her blind and muddle her words. My brother has surrounded himself with comics and has stayed in the rondavel. He won't even come into the house for lunch. Lally has spent most of the day with the new nanny Salome and the baby, and the rest of it washing and curling her hair, with my grandmother fussing about her with hairspray and plastic rollers. I no longer begrudge her those royal aspirations. My new allegiance is to the king. Even though I am a white girl with hair bleached fair in the sun, I have decided deep down I have a Swazi heart.

After lunch I wander up to the compound to find Martha who has disappeared after breakfast. I haven't been up to the compound since the day the Dad dragged me down and made me bath alone in the insect bath. That was months ago, and now the Dad has gone through to Malkerns to look at a new tractor for the pineapple farm.

I find Martha standing outside her room. She has her back to me, her hands on her hips, looking down as if she is talking to somebody small. As I come closer I am surprised to see it is Rahab, squatting down on her haunches with her back against the wall. She is looking down at the ground. Ruddy boot-polish patches shine on her cheeks where her tears have washed away a fine layer of dust that covers her skin like powder. She is wrapped in an orange patterned blanket. The fringe of beads has gone from her forehead, and she looks quite ordinary with a doek on her head like a maid. I move to Martha's side and grab onto her hand. She doesn't look at me at all, but carries on speaking quickly and quietly to her daughter. The urgency in her voice is of no comfort to Rahab because the tears still stream down her face, unchecked. She sniffs and shudders like you do when the crying starts and you just can't stop.

'What's wrong with Rahab?' I ask her later when we are in the kitchen together.

'She be sick, that Rahab.'

'Is that why she's crying?'

'Yes'um.'

'Is the doctor going to come?'

'Yes'um.'

Martha doesn't want to talk about Rahab.

She is mixing laundry starch into a jug of boiled water. I put my hand in the packet and drop some of the white granules onto my tongue. I love the way the starch sucks up all the spit in your mouth in a moment and dissolves into a sticky white film that you can barely swallow. It tastes of nothing.

'She going to stay with my sister in Big Bend.'
'But I thought she was going to get married in Zululand?'
'She be married later, yes.'

Martha never spoke about Rahab after that. If I tried to ask her again, she closed her mouth, pursed those lips and pretended she didn't hear.

Rahab went away the next day and only came back after Christmas, after the time of the fire.

Our Uncle Hugh never came back to visit us in Swaziland. We saw him again about five years later, a much older and changed man with a beard that hid half his face. In his eyes he carried a sad resignation, as if he bore the burden of undisclosed pursuits reluctantly in his heart, as if he'd lost his laughter and grown up at last.

We missed him. Thomas missed him.

VII

The day the holidays ended, my mother slipped a letter into Thomas's blazer pocket on his way back to boarding school. He never showed it to me. I found it one day a long time after Thomas had gone, slipped between the pages of his leopard scrapbook.

Uncle Hugh had written a poem especially for Thomas and the leopard. It was tucked into the letter on a separate piece of paper.

Shaba, The Leopard – a poem for Thomas by Hugh McMillan

'What name shall men call thee?
Osiris eyes of burning Amber worn upon thy back,
Watching shadows in the darkest black
Of night lit only by the stars
From whence Leo beckons Felis Pard.

And still the Ancient kings are wrapped around
In shades of gold and black and white,
Cloaked in humble sacrifice.
Dare men to know from whence
Arose thy Pard Magnificence?
Is it Cruelty that burns
Behind those orbs of marbled fire?
When the full-blood Magic Moon hangs still
Above the hushed Earth,
She waits and watches from her throne
Of Agate, Granite, Mountain Stone
And if be thee such Dreadful Beast that
Drags the weak upon the tree,
Who is this perfect Feline Queen
That reigns with grace her Sovereign Deity?
How shall men know thee?

Even though Thomas kept the letter a secret, he learnt the poem by heart and he would stand in his pyjamas beside his bed and recite it, just as Uncle Hugh would have, with the same earnest intonation and inflection. It was almost like a prayer, Thomas's prayer to the watcher of souls.

At night, when Thomas was home from school, he had begun to listen again at the window for the sound of the leopard returning. He found fresh paw prints in Gaga's rose beds once and swore me to secrecy. He told me that Shaba knew he waited for her, and that was why she kept coming back. He could feel her watching us from the mountain.

There were no more letters from Uncle Hugh. If there were, Thomas never received them.

My brother has become morose and indifferent since Uncle Hugh left, but the Dad does not give up on him. He seems to know that petty attempts to win him back at this stage are inconsequential, so he has plotted something much bigger, a scheme that even a disconsolate Thomas could never refuse. To win this game, the Dad refrains from addressing Thomas directly, but rather throws out his new bait at dinner, to a wider audience.

'I'm going down to Havelock on Saturday to see a good friend who works at the mines there. He has a light airplane he wants to show me.'

Thomas stops eating, he stares into the glass of water beside his plate.

'Might take her up for a bit of a spin. Anyone want to come up with me?'

Thomas rearranges his serviette on his lap. I try to capture his eyes with a hypnotic stare.

'We would be airsick, wouldn't we, Jilly?' said Mum.~ 'What about you, Thomas? You've always wanted to fly.'

'Oh, I don't know,' says the Dad, 'he might be bored around two ex-air force veterans. What about you, Papa?'

'Don't think so... can't risk it with my old ticker.'

Thomas is staring hard at what is left on his plate, considering his meagre options. If I concentrate hard enough I might fix his mind in a determined state of refusal. But it slips out of my grasp. This clearly needs Thomas's co-operation.

'I don't mind. If you need someone to go with you...' he says finally, and swallows down his excitement with a glass of water so the Dad doesn't think he is doing him a favour. All I have succeeded in doing is reading his thoughts, which are so predictable it's sickening.

It is that easy.

My brother and the Dad spend the day together, male bonding in a cockpit, and talking about the hair's-breadth-of-a-second-near-misses that make up the fond tales of bygone war heroes. When he returns that night his eyes sparkle, he is animated with heroic tales. The Dad is the centre of it all and sits there with a remote smile of amusement and smugness pushing up the corners of his moustache.

Dad says that when I'm older I can take flying lessons and become a pilot! Dad and Uncle Tosh fought together in the Second World War and Dad joined the air force when he was only seventeen! Dad was a gunner on a B52 and shot down zillions of enemy aircraft!

Weaving and unweaving the tangled thread of those times, I can see how Thomas's need overcame his common sense and integrity and split him down the middle like two halves of a walnut in the same shell.

VIII

The school year is rushing towards its finishing line like a frantic potato race. Mum's term calendar hangs on the back of the kitchen door and is plotted and circled and highlighted like a giant geography map. I am pleased she is a teacher again. In her organized mind, she stores all the dates for tests, eisteddfods, functions and festivals and that lifts the burden off my own mind, which is preoccupied with daydreams that have very little to do with school. Mrs Dawson has entered my name for the Summer Festival Art Competition and Thomas has auditioned for the Drama Eisteddfod.

I know Mum is proud of us both, though she isn't in the habit of bragging about her children in public. She says bragging is the wrong kind of pride and as such it is decidedly common. 'Common' is a word that covers all sorts of misdemeanours, like talking with a mouth full of bubble gum, ladies who wore too much make-up about their eyes, children dressed like Poorwhites, men with tattoos, ladies with high-pitched voices – and bragging in public.

Mum spends hours helping Thomas with voice production and gesture. She is training him to use his voice like an instrument. Just like music, she says, you need to discover the range of tones in your own speaking voice. Sometimes a voice can make people cry, just like an opera singer.

I'm not sure why she would want people to cry at the eisteddfod. No one would cry if I win or lose the art competition, unless it was me. Besides, crying in public is probably common. Gaga says: 'I won't have you snivelling in here. If you have to cry, go and do it quietly in your bedroom so we don't have to look at that miserable face.'

Thomas knows his poem with all the subtle inflections, pauses and gestures, and so do I by the time I've heard it for the hundredth time.

'Is anybody there?' said the Traveller,
Knocking on the moonlit door;
And his horse in the silence champed the grass
Of the forest's ferny floor...

The whole house echoes with the voice of the Traveller and the house stands still and listens with De La Mare's phantom listeners.

And he felt in his heart their strangeness,
Their stillness answering his cry.

Thomas has won a certificate of excellence for 'The Listeners'. The only one who cried at all was my mother, but I don't think anyone saw it but me. I think she was so proud she just couldn't hold it all in without a little spill. Mr Marshall, the headmaster, said Thomas should say his poem at Parents Evening, on the last day of school, he was that pleased with him.

The only one who doesn't care for the poem at all is the Dad. He says poetry is for queers, and he always finds some excuse not to be in the lounge when Thomas steps from the plum velvet curtains onto the silk carpet stage. Neither my brother nor I know what 'queers' means. We think he's invented the word as a good excuse not to be there.

No one in the family has yet seen the painting I made for the Art Competition. This time we weren't allowed to draw something from our imaginations. We were each given a slip of a fruit tree or a flowering shrub to copy. We could draw it or paint it, or use colour crayons. I took my two sable brushes with me and the watercolour tubes Uncle Hugh had brought me, and a small porcelain saucer from Gaga's kitchen.

Mine is a slip from a lemon tree. The lemons are still small and sour green, so almost everything on the desk is green, except the knobbly wood bark itself. But I am learning to look past those first impressions. Mrs Dawson's voice plays in my head: Look carefully, Jilly, there's so much more. My desk is close to the window and daylight spills through the leaves and onto the lemons. I sit there with my hands in my lap and stare without blinking.

I see it all in a moment, perfect shapes that fit together to make a nameless whole. It is all light and shadow, and shapes of every subtle hue of green, from violet to white.

I lose myself in that place until I feel Mrs Dawson's hand touch my shoulder. I almost forget I am making a picture of leaves and lemons until I recognise it there on the paper and she says:

'Oh, Jilly!... Yes!... Yes!'

Like an answer to a question we've both asked.

As I walk down the corridor, past empty classrooms with empty chairs, my head is dizzy with the joy that remains like a lingering aftertaste. This is a knowing that springs from the heart, felt rather than thought. In retrospect, I suppose it was that absolute certainty that real art is immeasurable, that all it took was to be in that place where the shapes and names of things didn't matter, where you come to be the things you see.

But it is so difficult to shape that certainty with words. I know. I know something, but I don't know exactly what it is. I can't wait to try and explain it to my mother. She has the right words for everything.

I've quite forgotten that Angus, my mother's Morris Minor, is at the garage, petered out. I remember when I see the Dad's jeep in the school parking lot. He is standing with one foot on the running step, drumming impatiently on the roof. I climb into the back and wait for Mum to come out the front portals of the school. The Dad ignores me at first, then thinks better of it and settles into the driver's seat.

'Why're you all so late?' he asks.

'It was the art thing today.'

'Huh…'

'When I grow up I'm going to be a real artist.'

'Uh-huh…'

'… seeing as I can't be a royal princess.'

'Where's your mother?'

'Dunno.'

When Mum arrives, laden down with books and bags, the Dad says nothing, punishing her with silence. As the jeep drives away my mother reaches her hand round the back of the seat and finds mine. She squeezes it in secret. It's her way of saying, 'I know you're there' without the words. I squeeze it back. 'I know you do.' Like an Indian smoke message.

When the Dad is in one of his moods it's safer to keep feelings buried. A wordless quiet is better than a silence broken. When he breaks it himself, just before we turn into the drive, his anger cuts through the stillness like breaking glass.

'Can't wait to get out of this place! It's bloody suffocating.'

My mother stiffens.

'She's lying there like a beached whale on her bed, under a cloud of impending doom.'

'Who is?'

'Your mother.'

'What's wrong?'

'What's wrong? How do I know what's wrong? I expect it's that damn queer brother of yours stirring up trouble. Even from over there he can't keep his mouth shut. And it's not as if I don't have other things on my plate.'

He stops the car in front of the house.

'Do you know what I have on my plate?'

Grown-ups use imaginary plates to carry around their troubles.

'What do you mean?'

'You don't have a clue, do you?'

'Bryan, please…We'll talk about this later.' My mother indicates that I am still in the back seat.

He laughs bitterly and bangs his fists down on the steering wheel.

'Jilly, get out the car.' My mother's voice is taught and sharp.

'But I wanted…'

'Get out now.'

I slam the door just hard enough to let it speak my anger for me.

I creep into my grandparents' room and find my grandmother lying supine on the bed, a damp facecloth covering her forehead. Her face is pale and dry like creased linen. All the paint on her bird-beak lips has slipped off the edges. I cover her hands with mine and she stirs.

'Gillian?'

'Uh-hu.'
'I'm so tired, dear.'
'What's the matter?'
'I don't know, but something is. It's the dreams coming again.' She heaves the air in under her wide bosom and then sighs and fills the room with it.

I pat her hand as if I understand.
'Do you need tea?' Tea is always a comfort.
'No, dear, I'll just lie here for a while.'

I leave the room quietly. Outside the air is still and heavy. Like there should be a storm on the way, but there are no clouds at all.

IX

'Hamba tata lo spade, Solomon – Gahle, gahle, don't trample on the beds! What's the matter with you people?'

As much as PapaMac's domain is his vegetable garden, my grandmother's pleasure is in the flowers that proliferate under her tender care throughout the year. It's the only reason she began to learn her limited snatches of Swazi. It's really Fanagalo, the Dad says, the language they communicate in across the eleven tribes that work side by side in the gold mines of Johannesburg.

Afternoons find Gaga wandering through her garden beds in gum boots and a wide straw hat and rough linen gloves, throwing out the odd instruction in Fanagalo to Solomon who follows her along the borders with a keen ear lest she come down on him in one of her bitter rages.

'Tata lo watering can, and tela manzi lapa – Hayikona wena! Not like that, Solomon… Don't these people ever understand?'

Then there is the musical language of flowers and gardening, the strange repartee shared between mothers. It is one area of common ground in which my mother and grandmother bond and blossom together. The language of gardening is strung out like beaded love letters across the black soil, mulch, prune, pluck, dibber, cultivars, rhizomes, rosettes, succulents... I often follow the two mothers around the beds, just to repeat the lyrical names and roll them around my tongue, a sweet and scented taste.

That Saturday after the art competition my mother walks the flower beds with her mother, and me following invisibly, three generations of females in a garden. They stop at shrubs and perennials, herbs and annuals, exclaiming with delight and surprise at the colours, the new blooms, stroking the petals of this one and smelling a pinch of that. English roses planted amongst French lavender, gypsophila amongst the tulips from Amsterdam, azalea shrubs and blue and pink heads of Christmas flowers as big as plates.

Pansies and petunias are planted along the edges with a sprinkle of alyssum and black clover. There were tall hollyhocks and agapanthus against a lattice fence that is trailed with sweet jasmine and black-eyed Susans. Dahlias, zinnias, rosemary and one-day lilies, so many of them the names of girls, like mine. There could easily be gillians growing somewhere in the dark soil of Swaziland, smiling up at the sun. Me multiplied in miniature.

My mother loves the fluorescent mesembryanthemums, growing round the rockery like sea anemones. Mesembryanthemum... Mum-the-Bryan-mesem... a whispered breathy sound like a witch's spell.

My favourites are the snapdragons. They have lilac and purple jaws you can snap open and shut with your fingers. Delicate and harmless dragons that feed on sun-filled days and misty nights, and end up in glass vases on the French-polished tables in the lounge.

Mum is choosing some flowers for Parents Evening on Tuesday.

She asks Gaga which ones would look best together to make a fine arrangement for the school hall. Gaga looks a lot better in the sunshine, as if the flowers have reached up and touched her cheeks with colour. She stoops to cut some hydrangeas that I guess are for our hall table.

'When will you be leaving?' she asks over her shoulder.

'Bryan will be going up mid-January and we'll follow, probably a couple of weeks later.'

'It's so far away. I'll worry about you.'

'I know, but we have to get on with our own lives, Mum, we can't live with you forever.'

Gaga sighs. 'We'll miss you.'

Of course I've known it, like a bedtime story, like tidal waves in Japan and Jack the Ripper. But the certainty of it hits me in the face like a wet cloth. It is coming true, just like Thomas said. You can't live with other people forever. They'd said that we were going to Rhodesia, but they'd often told us things that belonged to some future place and time, abstract things that never came true.

I wander up the lawn and take the path towards the rondavel. You can't live with other people. Other people meant Gaga and Papa, Martha and Solomon, even Lally. Change is inevitable, can't hold it back. Panic spreads through me, coursing through my legs, my feet, my fingers. I lie on my bed and bury my head in the pillow, breathing in the familiarity of my grandmother's clean, ironed linen and the smell of the Swazi sun.

That night, I dream I am leaping over rocks, like a sure-footed klipspringer, while the waters swirl in troubled torrents around me. Royal scarlet feathers rush past me, carried along on the surface too quickly for me to save even one. If I could only catch one, the water would freeze in a moment and turn to bronze, and there stands the bronze fisher-boy, open mouthed, staring with surprise because at the end of his copper fishing line there is nothing at all. Thomas is blowing air in my face and it smells of toothpaste. It is middle-of-the-night dark in the room with the bathroom light off, but the half-moon light filters through the fabric of the curtains. It strikes me how black Thomas looks against the sheet, against the light of the white lemon slice moon. Do we all look the same colour in the dark? Thomas pulls me up, hushing me in soft whispers. He takes my hand and leads me to the chair next to the window. The night is deathly quiet; even the crickets are singing in muted trills. The moon hangs in a silky haze behind thin swathes of mist, the earth's warm breath touching the cool night. I am not sure what I'm supposed to be looking at.

Listen, Thomas whispers close to my cheek. His hair has that distinctive boy smell, sweat and pepper.

The night reaches out its stillness like an empty bowl. Just the mindless trill of cricket conversation, a sound so familiar in Africa, like your own breathing.

Then Thomas squeezes my hand and I hear it too. A harsh rasping cry, repeated like a saw cutting a branch. It is followed by a strange coughing sound. Then it stops.

'What was that?' I whisper.

'It's Shaba. She's out there. It's hard to tell exactly where, but that's a leopard call, I know.'

'How do you know?'

'I've heard it before, that night...'

There it is again. It's impossible to know how far away she is, but her harsh cry has spilt its secret down the hill, through the tall wild grass and sickle bush, along the stone granite ground, over sleeping shrubs and shadowy perennials, towards the house, then up into the quiet leaves of the gum trees where the eagle owls watch and shudder. Thomas seems to breathe in the sound, as if it were uttered in particular to sustain him. She calls repeatedly, four, perhaps five times and Thomas listens, unmoving, arrested, as if in that strange rasping call she speaks a sacred ineffable truth.

It is turning away from us. Then it's gone.

We wait at the window, thoughts like kites flying away from us, upward, until the string snaps and a silk shape spirals out of the black nowhere, and the green-yellow wings of a moon moth flutter against the window and startle us. It settles on the glass, as big as my hand.

'Look, it has four eyes,' says Thomas.

'It looks like a kite with two tails.'

'Never follow the moon moth,' says Thomas. 'It'll lead you to the place of witches.'

'Stoppit.'

'Martha said they steal children for muti.'

'Moon moths?'

'No, witches.'

The moon moth has floated off into the darkness, and we climb back into our beds.

'I wonder if anyone else heard the leopard?' I say.

'No,' says Thomas.

'I wonder if we should tell.'

'What's the point?'

Thomas is no longer interested in sharing our leopard with anyone, as if their doubt would somehow break the intangible magic of her presence. Something rare and autonomous is growing between him and that elusive creature, something I cannot begin to understand.

X

Baby Essie is barely visible, wrapped in a cocoon of blankets strapped tightly to Martha's back. Martha is making an upside-down cake in the kitchen and I am perched on a high cane stool waiting to lick the bowl and pick at the bits of tinned fruit left behind. Martha hasn't been quite the same since Rahab returned and went to stay with her sister in Big Bend. I do not try to break through her reluctance to talk about her daughter or the Zulu wedding that was waiting to happen in the future; it is not worth risking her obstinate silence. I tell her instead that we are going away in January to live in Rhodesia. I say it in a way that is designed to punish her for being a grown-up, and for not being able to stop it. I turn my resentment upon her, because she is more accessible than the others and I want her to share in the heaviness I feel pressing down on my own heart.

'We're going forever and we won't come back here ever again.'

'One day you'll come back, Miss Jilly. Forever is too long.'

'It'll be forever, you'll see.'

'Inkhulunkhulu will decide when forever begins and ends.'

'Even God knows you can't live with other people forever. Anyway, I'm too old to have a nanny.'

She looks up at me.

'Ntombazane,' she says softly.

The tears I have been holding back for so long burst forth. She opens her arms for me and holds me in a smothering embrace until I have to stop and come up for air.

'A child who does not cry dies slowly on her mother's back. It is good to cry, Miss Jilly, and speak what you have inside in your heart.'

'I don't want to go.'

'I know this.'

She pushes the mixing bowl towards me and I dip my fingers into the stickiness of the cake batter and lick the vanilla sweetness until there is nothing left.

Drawing pictures now becomes a practical incantation to ward off the unknowable future and contain the world in a space that is familiar and unchanged. I draw the shapes of Gaga's garden, the jacaranda trees that shade the lawn, the house with its thatched roof hat and double chimneys. Papa and Gaga stand at the door. I draw the chickens behind the wire mesh (hard to capture on paper, they look more like ducks), the four green doors of the compound and the big Tamboti tree that grows into the sky like a wide umbrella. I draw the smiling sun huge and yellow, its rays like fingers drying the laundry that Martha has hung on a giant washing line. Grey mountains are shaded in pencil against a dark sky where the full moon hangs, and in the shadows of the mountain rocks a leopard (that looks more like a dog) is barely visible against the smudged graphite background. But my faith in the power of imagination and the artist's wand is diminishing. I am no longer sure. The power to keep things as they are is no longer quite as convincing.

XI

Whatever it was that caused Thomas to change his mind that night, we never found out. But we all packed into the six-seater lounge of Papa's Pontiac and drove down Malagwane hill and into Mbabane to wait in patient tolerance of the 'common' crowds that were sardine-squeezed into the St Mark's Junior hall, simply to hear my brother's final deliverance of 'The Listeners' by Walter de la Mare. Even the Dad came, having slicked his hair back with Brylcreem and lost himself for a while in a couple of glasses of whisky before we left.

Thomas stood in the middle of the stage, unexpectedly small and pale. Hesitant. The pause was too long and there was an impatient shuffle from the audience, and I closed my eyes and willed him to remember the words we all knew so well. Then his voice filled the hall with surprise.

'I won't be doing that poem,' he said. 'I have chosen to do another one instead. It's called Shaba, and it was written by my uncle, Hugh MacMillan.'

He began slowly, his voice boldly resonating through the silent hall.

What shall men call thee? Osiris eyes of burning amber...

There it is, unshadowed and exposed, the spoken evidence of our wandering feline beast. Our Leopard-on-the-hill... in the garden... in the scrapbook...

It is beautiful, like music, like colours rich and the smell of wild things. My Thomas. Our Shaba.

A storm of clapping and thunderous stamping of feet on the wooden floor carries Thomas up into the rafters of stage lights and into the realms of stardom. It isn't just the poem. They would have extolled him for a nursery rhyme well rendered, he is that popular amongst his peers, a mentor to the juniors. Everyone knows Thomas Woods.

Only the Dad sits stony and silent on the back seat of the Pontiac on the way home. He would not grant my mother even the pretence of pleasure. For once everyone ignores his petulance and he bears it impassively on the periphery of our insouciant bliss. I should have known, though, that our bliss couldn't last in the bright light of day.

In the morning, at final assembly, anguish is written on my mother's pinched face as she sits there on the stage with the other teachers. Even my gold-edged certificate with my name emblazoned there in perfect script for the painting of green lemons wins less respite from her weary resignation than it should have. There is to be no more mention of the leopard or our Uncle Hugh. The Dad is in no mood to hear another word about it. Promise me, she says, just to keep the peace.

So we promise. There are so many promises to keep the peace after that we lose count of them and lies and secrets self-seed like the marigolds that grow like weeds amongst Gaga's perennials.

PART FOUR

Fire

The smell of methylated spirits greets us from the front door. The freshly cleaned glass cabinet doors are open in the lounge and my grandmother is carefully wrapping her porcelain ladies in butcher's paper and placing them in cardboard boxes on the floor.

'Why're you packing them away?' I ask, hoping she'll say they are coming with us to Rhodesia.

'Just to keep them safe.'

'Safe from what?'

'From the calamity.'

'What's a calamity?'

Mum hurried us into the kitchen to make sandwiches for lunch.

'What's a calamity?' I ask her.

'Never mind the old dear. She dreams things.'

'Are you pleased with my picture of lemons?'

My mother puts her hand up to her mouth as if she's just remembered.

'I'm so proud of you, darling.'

'It was all there. All of a sudden.'

'What was, dear?'

'The lemons and the light.'

'It's beautiful.'

'Like I saw it for the first time.'

'You're so clever. Both of you.'

'I can't really explain it in words.'

'That's why you're an artist, I expect. You explain it best on paper. Without words.'

Is she right? Do I explain it best without words?

'I want to give it to Gaga,' I say, 'for her calamity.'

'That's nice, dear.'

Thomas has disappeared into the garden and left his school clothes in a pile on the rondavel floor. I pick them up to save them from the scorpions, and dump them on his pillow. Ahead of us is the longest holiday of the year, and I want to stretch the time to make it last forever. Time goes slower when you do nothing and expect something. I lie down on my bed and gaze up at the thatch watching lizard time. Sometimes those lizards just hang there upside-down, invisible glue on their gummy feet. A lizard can stay in one place for hours, and time stands still with the waiting.

As the afternoon light slipped away behind the mountains, the birds became restless and scattered upwards and away down the valley as though they shared a secret visceral language of their own. The presentiment of the 'calamity' was not limited to the eccentricities of my grandmother's intuitive dreaming. Ziggie, Papa's faithful old Alsatian, acted upon an instinctive urging and crept into the lounge and hid behind Gaga's floral couch. But even in the emptiness and silence of an evening sky, Gaga lying in a darkening bedroom with her porcelain ladies, the outside dog inside behind the couch, and Baby Essie's fretful crying, the rest of the family remained oddly oblivious to the approaching fire. The clouds that settled over the mountains were grey and heavy, a perfect camouflage for the smoke rising up to meet them. By the time the warning came from Mr Pilkins, our neighbour, and the ghostly siren split the evening quiet, the fire had crept down the hill and was almost upon us.

It's the sound of the siren that wakes me. Now I stand at the rondavel door with sleep and confusion buzzing through my head. There are strange people rushing through our garden and trampling through Gaga's flowers, pulling hosepipes and shouting. I see my mother at the kitchen door, holding baby Essie on her hip with one hand and waving with the other – a frantic conductor of an orchestra. Then I realise she is waving at me. Her hand says, Stay where you are! Her mouth is shaping words but her voice is drowning in the waves of the siren. The men lift the hosepipes upwards and begin to spray the thatched roof. Now my mother's lips mouth the same word over and over. 'You must! You must!' Everything is so absurd, I think I'm sleep-walking. I look back into the rondavel for a second, almost expecting to see Thomas sitting on the bed grinning. But there is no one there and I suddenly feel the heat of panic rising in my chest. I run across the path towards my mother, through the chaos of people and hose-pipes. She pulls me against her and backs into the kitchen, and it is then I realise that she's been calling Thomas!

'Where's Thomas?' she says throwing her voice at me, higher than normal pitch.

'What's happening?'

'There's a fire coming down the hill. Gillian, look at me! Where's Thomas?'

'You left me all alone in the rondavel!'

'Martha saw you were sleeping. It's going to be all right.'

She grips my shoulder and shakes me.

'Please, darling. Do you know where Thomas is?'

The wail of the siren suddenly stops. My mother's voice is desperately loud.

'I don't know.'

I know I've made things worse by crying.

'Dammit, I wish your father was here.'

I wish he was too, because everything is going wrong. But of course she means the new Dad, not the one in England.

'Give Baby to me, Ma'am. It's better to go find Thomas.'

Martha has been standing behind us. She takes Essie from my mother's arms and slides her onto her back, tying the blanket in a knot around her waist. I hold Martha's hand and watch Mum run back into the passage, stricken with the energy of panic. For the first time I smell the burning of veld grass on the air. A hot wind blows through the kitchen door and the smell begins to creep through the house.

'If we stay here we'll all burn!' I say.

Baby Essie is crying now. Martha closes the back door.

'Better to stay right here,' she says.

'Who are all those people?'

'From the farm location. Mr Pili-kins' boys.'

There are farm locations in Malkerns where Lally lives, small clusters of square houses, bigger than our compound, where the natives live with their children and chickens, goats and mielies all on top of each other. We've seen the location piccaninnies from the next-door farm swimming naked in the dam over the hill.

From the window, Martha and I watch the water drip from the roof and the puddles growing deep on the cement courtyard outside the kitchen. The men from the location hoist the hoses away from the house and begin to soak the roof of the rondavel. Smoke rises above the rondavel roof, a white smudge on the darkening sky. Charred threads float and eddy in the air, like pitch snow.

'I'm going to find my Gaga.'

I pull away from Martha and run into the passage, past the dining room with the table already set for dinner and into the lounge. The whole house is deathly quiet, dimly lit by the final glow of an evening sky through the windows. There is no electricity. My mother has gone. Only the old dog lies shivering in a corner behind the couch.

I open the door to the grandparents' room. She is lying on her back again, a rug pulled up to her chin. At the foot of the bed are several cardboard boxes. She lies there like an Egyptian Mummy, the treasures of her life buried in her pyramid tomb with her, to take her to the other side. My Tutankhamen granny.

For a second I convince myself that she is dead.

Then she stirs.

'I knew it was coming. He's never believed in the dreaming,' she says.

The smell of burning has already seeped into the room.

'Is this the calamity?'

'The house will be all right. Need to find Thomas now. He can't find his way home.'

'Where is he?'

'That place where the natives live.'

'But where?'

'I don't know, dear.'

'Will he be all right?'

'He's frightened.'

When I open the front door, I find the Dad's jeep parked outside in the drive with the lights still on and the doors open. I stumble back into the darkness of the hall, running my fingers along the walls. I find my way to the veranda and slip out onto the damp lawn. I run around the side of the house and bump into Solomon carrying two zinc buckets full of water. I grab onto his sleeve.

'Tell me where the natives live.'

'Get into the house, Miss Jilly.'

'No, Solomon. You must tell me. Thomas is there!' I am screaming at him as if we are valleys apart.

He bends down and looks into my face. Black pearls of sweat shine on his forehead.

'He's not be at the compound, Jilly.'

'It's not the compound. It's another place where...'

'The location? You think the location?'

'I think so...'

'You stay, Missy. I go for Thomas.'

He leaves me standing there, my teeth chattering from cold or fear, it doesn't matter. I walk up to the kitchen courtyard and stand in the puddles watching numbly as the black silhouettes of warriors beat the flames that lick the edges of the kikuyu lawn, just yards away from the insect bathroom. The fire is a living thing transforming itself as it moves, a scarlet dragon with mouthless tongues feeding greedily on anything that lies in its path. Somewhere behind me I hear the sound of a car starting up, then gravel scattered by the rush of tires on the drive. I feel someone grab me roughly from behind and push me into the candle-lit kitchen, where Mum and PapaMac, Martha and Patience hug the shadows. They are railing me with a thousand questions that hum on the bitter stench of burning. Dizziness rings in my ears, so that their words jostle together without meaning.

I say: 'Thomas is all right. Solomon went to find him.'

'Dad's taken him in the jeep.' My mother's face is up against my own.

'He's frightened, Mum.'

'It'll be O.K.'

Martha shakes her head, 'Aye, bathu!'

'The fire's under control now. Everything's going to be all right,' PapaMac says.

II

The boy that walked into the house that night is a ghost of the boy I know as my brother.

Under the streaks of black soot his face is pale as a cold moon. His knees are scraped and grazed and he shivers, jelly-boned, chilled with cold and shock. Our mother bathes us in the big bath in the house, scrubbing the black ash from our faces and hair. She dabs mercurochrome on my brother's knees and elbows which are scraped raw from his adventure. Martha has made sweet tea and sandwiches, but no one eats much. Everything tastes like burnt toast. Thomas and I sleep in the lounge, falling into our dreams the minute our heads touch the pillows.

We wake up parched and coughing like trench-troop smokers, with the acrid taste of burnt grass in our mouths. A fine soot dust covers everything. The dining table and all the porcelain plates are dusted with it and scattered sprinkles of charred offerings, unrecognisable bits of leaf and bark and grass. We've had to wash our nostrils and gargle with salt water, and Martha has made us sip freshly squeezed orange juice, but still the taste stays with us.

Outside my grandmother is weeping for her trampled flowers and singed shrubs. Half the kikuyu lawn above the kitchen is scorched, and behind the insect bathroom the wall is blackened and the lower eaves of thatch singed. It was that close.

Mum says that Thomas and I are going to spend a few days with Lally. With all the cleaning we would only get under their feet. Everything in the house must be cleaned, vacuumed and dusted. It could take them days, washing curtains, linen and clothes and crockery; even the walls are pale grey. Only the treasures like the porcelain ladies, the paintings, Italian vases and bronze sculptures are safely wrapped and untouched by the devastation. Gaga says 'Thank

God for that' to no one in particular and Papa is too weary to reply. He sits at the kitchen table sipping tea and staring out the door, his lips tinged a pale blue.

The Dad drives us to Malkerns in the jeep. It is Thomas's punishment to be ignored. Completely. The Dad refers everything he says to me, which isn't much anyway. Have you got your toothbrush? Remember your manners at Auntie Sylvia's house. Don't go round barefoot, and no playing near the farm compound.

Thomas says, 'How long do we have to stay there?'

'We'll fetch you in a few days,' he says to me, as if Thomas isn't there. It was the same when he fetched Thomas last night from the location. It was Solomon who wrapped him in his jacket. The Dad sat in stony silence all the way back. When they got to the house, Thomas said, the Dad told him he deserved nothing but a good thrashing. If you were my son... That was all.

Lally is standing in her drive when we arrive. She is so happy to see us, she dances around the car like a fairy with long legs and braces. The Dad speaks to Auntie Sylvia while we pull our suitcases inside. By the time we come out again, the jeep is gone.

Thomas and I don't really know our Auntie that well. There are secrets the grown-ups whisper about Lally's parents, Thomas says, and Gaga doesn't much like our Auntie Sylvia because 'some women drive their men to drink'. So, we have only met her in passing, usually when she drops Lally at the house or picks her up again. To me she's just Lally's mother, and I am not at all pleased to be at Lally's, having come into this world with an innate suspicion of any place I haven't lived in for a few months at least. But Thomas seems quite relaxed as usual, chatting to our aunt as if he's spent a lifetime getting to know her.

Our lunch of fishcakes and fried chips is a feast for the famished.

Thomas and I are ravenous for anything that doesn't taste of charcoal, and I forget that I'm a sworn vegetarian.

'Bring us some tea, Ousie, with a little condensed milk. These kids are starving!'

A sombre black girl drifts in and out the kitchen as if she is hovering backstage at a performance, moving the props about and hoping not to be noticed.

'Now, tell me all about it, honey. Spill the beans. And don't leave anything out. I want to hear the whole bang-shoot.'

My brother needs no more encouragement than that! Centre stage of a catastrophe is the best place for Thomas to be in the theatre of his eleven-year-old life.

The way he speaks of the fire, you might have imagined he'd staged the whole event single-handed. In fact, the thought has crossed my mind, but it is too dreadful to pursue. There is no doubt what he was doing out there in the bush, though. He tells Auntie Sylvia he was out hunting for scorpions and lost track of time. Better to lie about that, than have another grown-up turn away in disbelief at the real reason.

I watch Lally and her mother fuss and pout and gesture over Thomas. My cousin is a carbon copy of her mother, every turn of phrase and arrangement of hands, except that my aunt is larger. Much larger. Shaped like a pear, her narrow shoulders top a wide and expanding midriff and below her skirt, stockinged balloon legs that end in tiny neat feet shoed in heels that defy the natural laws of balance. And her hair is brighter than Lally's, the colour of lemon curd and worn in undulating waves around her face. Her mouth is wide with lips painted on in shiny ruby red, and even though she isn't going anywhere, her eyelids are smudged with the same colour as the blue-headed lizards that live in our garden rockery. But she is kind and attentive, and in the few days we are there she mothers us tenderly and incessantly, especially me, because I am the youngest, and that is more than a year's worth of mothering at home. We say prayers before every meal and when she tucks us under the bedclothes at night she prays away unimaginable horrors and hugs us in warm lemon smells and leaves our cheeks stained with ruby kisses. There is neither sight nor sound of Uncle George, no trace of a man amongst the cotton lace doilies, the pink sateen curtains, the rose-edged china tea cups. It is as if he's never been there at all.

It is only when the three of us are alone that Thomas tells us about the Leopard.

Did he really see her?

Thomas says he did. He found her on the other side of the valley, there on the mountain, on the edge of the gorge where three massive granite boulders balance precariously above a sharp drop that cuts through to the scrub below. You can see it from the top of our hill. Even I know the place. He says he didn't know why, it was that particular place that seemed to draw him, as if he somehow knew she'd be there. At a certain point he looked up and there she was, just as he knew she would be. She lay there above him on the ledge of granite. There were two young cubs, he said, playing about, only visible now and again. She looked down at Thomas. She had probably been watching his careful approach for hours.

They'd looked steadily into each other's eyes, Thomas and his leopardess. A moment that seemed like forever, he said.

Was he scared?

He shrugs and closes his eyes.

'I thought: she could kill me right now. And suddenly I wasn't scared. It didn't matter.'

Then she rose up slowly. And she was gone. It was only then that Thomas turned to look down the valley and saw the fire spilling into the thatching grass between him and the way home.

He had to wait for the wind to shift before he could make it across the scorched veld towards the Pilkins' farm location. He had to wait for over an hour. He ran over the blackened ground as fast as he could, burning the soles of his takkies, kicking up the ash and embers and covering his face with his sleeves. He leapt over the last part that was still burning, closing his eyes because the fire was so hot he couldn't keep them open for the smarting. That was when he took a tumble, grazing his hands and knees on the rocks, black as the grass stubble and griddle-hot to the touch.

When he finally reached the whitewashed houses of the location he was streaked with soot and so thirsting for water he could barely speak. There were only two women there and a handful of young children. All the others were already at our house fighting the fire. The older woman fetched Thomas some water, while the younger one, swollen and heavily pregnant, tried to clean his scraped and bleeding knees. The children stood around him in the dust laughing at his charcoal face and singed hair. Most of them were naked, potbellied with inside-out belly buttons. Thomas might have laughed back, but he was bruised and too exhausted to care about anything but his own discomfort. His eyes were red rimmed and weeping of their own accord, washing away the stinging dryness from the smoke, so my brother says.

III

Most of the chickens died from asphyxiation. PapaMac told Solomon to take them, dump them, eat them, he didn't care as long as they were discarded. They would have to be replaced with semi-grown pecking chicks and we would be buying our eggs from the market in Mbabane for a while, and slaughtered chickens from the farm co-op for our dinners. Nothing much he could do about the garden or Gaga's trembling chin as she stared grimly at her ravaged love: just rake out the mess and start again. Papa employed another native boy to help with all the cleaning of the garden and the repainting of the outside wall of our rondavel. Everything had to be finished by Christmas, now only ten days away.

By the time Thomas and I returned from Lally's lace and lemon home, the house was perfectly clean and soot free. Just the windows of the lounge and dining room stood open-mouthed and undressed, gaping at the sweet kikuyu lawn that had remained, on this side at least, a contented green. The birds, wood pigeons and starlings, had come back and brought friends to roost and gossip on the thatched roof hat of Little Ezulwini. The business of mopping up, scrubbing down and cleaning had generated a frenetic energy in the household, and my brother and I caught it like a virus, running circles round the garden while the days stretched out in measured tides till Christmas.

Thomas and I have a generous assortment of old clothes and worn-out toys, books too young for us, and half-coloured colouring books and coverless comics useless for swapping. Mum has taken out the better things for our own natives and put aside the rest for the location at Pilkins' farm. She says we can take a drive there and deliver them ourselves in Angus, the Morris Minor, because the Dad has taken the jeep to Rhodesia for the week.

He has promised our mother he'll be back before Christmas. Meanwhile, it's better for all of us that he's left. He still hasn't spoken to Thomas since the fire, and dinner times have become staged events of hollowed-out silences, interrupted only by the clinking of cutlery against the plates and the sharp sound of the brass-skirted bell. He tried ineffectually to lose his morose disposition at the bottom of more than several whisky glasses before dinner. Normally this renders him acceptably effusive and inoffensive, but the suffocation of this place was obviously more than he could put up with.

Just five days before Christmas, my mother drives Angus over the dirt roads and up the scorched hill, and through the citrus orchards to where Pilkins' natives live. The car is packed to the brim with old curtains, unused skeins of wool, out of date jackets and skirts and other oddments that won't be travelling with us to our new home in Rhodesia. Thomas and I sit on top and in the midst of all the paraphernalia, laughing because our heads keep bumping on the cream ceiling of the car every time we hit a ditch or hump in the road.

When we arrive we are immediately surrounded by half-naked children, dusty brown, the colour of ginger biscuits. Pilkins' head farm boy, Petrus, distributes the sad second-hand remnants into a dustbowl of squabble; we are thanked with curtsies, clapping of hands and unrestrained laughter. Thomas has found the old woman that fetched him water when he'd run from the fire. He gives her Mum's cast-off knitted shawl in exchange for a wry smile she has saved for days like this. He asks Petrus where the other girl is, the one with the big belly, he indicates with his hands. Petrus laughs and shrugs off the question as if it is too much to bother with. We put the rest of the oddments down on the ground and let them sort it out between themselves. Mum gives Petrus a paper bag stuffed with Baby Essie's tiniest clothes.

'For the other one,' she says, 'that helped the boy when the fire came.'

We climb back into Angus and sing carols all the way home. Mum says that the spirit of Christmas is in the giving, and she's right. It warms your heart to give to the needy amid all that curtsying and nodding. Like when Gaga threw the coins to the piccaninnies that sang 'Jingle Bells' on the lawn of the Southbroom Hotel. We expected them to curtsy before our second-hand gifts. We expected nothing less.

IV

I think that the best gift for my mother would be all my treasures that I've hidden in my special place in the garden. All I need is a box to put them in, or a biscuit tin I could cover in the sixpence sheets of angel stickers I found at Mohammed's General Store.

I know Martha is having her tea up at the compound. I know she hoards things like biscuit tins in her khaya.

The door is shut from the inside with the brick, and behind the blistering green-painted wood, there is a low murmur of voices. I smack on the door with the palms of my hands. The murmuring stops, but no one answers. There is the smallest crack in the wood and I put my eye to it. I can only make out half of Martha's face, just half a nose and a staring eye, lit perhaps by the light of a candle. She seems to stare directly back at my eye looking in.

'Martha, it's me!' I call, shrinking back from the door. I am Walter de la Mare's Traveller waiting for the Listeners to reply. Tell them I came and no one answered!

'Is there anybody there?'

There is a scuffle from inside and she opens the door. Her wide girth obliterates my view of her visitors and the grim expression on her face prohibits any questions.

'I need a biscuit tin.'

'I bring you one now-now, Miss Jilly. I'm busy.'

'Okay. I'll wait.'

'No. No waiting.'

'But why?'

'You go back to the house, please.'

I turn and drag my shoes across the stone path towards the house. I am unaccustomed to Martha's dismissal of me. She has hardly said a word to me since the fire. Her patience wears thin at the slightest provocation these days, and even her usual household chores draw sighs from her and a shadow of displeasure. What is she hiding in her khaya anyway? The trust between us has begun to tarnish like old brass, my absolute dependence on her falters, and for the first time I feel alien in her world.

I don't belong up there at the compound.

Black people, white people, there is a valley between us.

V

Lally is to stay with us on the night before Christmas, and our Uncle George and Auntie Sylvia will be coming to share our Christmas lunch. That is when Lally tells us about Uncle George's Disgrace.

We have taken the stone path past the rondavel that leads down to the vegetable garden where PapaMac and Solomon have planted a miniature farmland of vegetables in neat and precise rows. Papa measures the spaces between the seedlings with a ruler, and flattens the earth to perfection with a spirit level, he is that particular about his garden.

Where we stand now, the mint has grown in wayward abundance under the garden tap, interspersed with white arum lilies with their wide goblet mouths and yellow tongues pointing rudely towards heaven.

'My Daddy's a disgrace because he can't keep his nose out the bottle, and PapaMac is ashamed of him,' she says. 'Ma says it's because of the war and his missing leg. He left half his leg in Italy and he drinks to forget the pain of losing it.'

He lives in Jo'burg most of the time and hardly ever comes to Swaziland. That's why we've hardly ever seen him.

'He only comes here to see me,' she says.

'Well, our Dad never comes to see us,' says Thomas. 'He's forgotten us.'

But this Christmas there is a card from our own Dad and his new wife. It comes all the way from England. In it he has written a short note: Saw Hugh the other day. He tells me you are both growing up and looking fine. I miss you. Perhaps one day... and that's how it ends, like he's forgotten to finish the last sentence. There is also a postcard from Uncle Hugh to all of us. Cambridge is freezing and they are expecting snow. He asks if we have received his letters, and writes that he'll be back for a visit in February and can't wait to see us all. He obviously hasn't heard about us leaving for Rhodesia. The picture on the front is of an old church that looks like a castle in the snow.

The keen thrill of Christmas Eve makes the whole world smile. We can hardly sleep, with shining promises hanging brightly in the warm night air. The stars, the trees and the lawns are heavy with expectation. It whispers into our dreams and nudges us into fitful states of restlessness, so that when the first light of dawn is a mere suggestion behind the curtains, we are awake.

My mother has never been inclined to enlarge upon tales of Father Christmas and other childish fancies. She's too busy carrying the burdens of the real world on her shoulders to bother with such trifles. Besides, we know all our gifts arrive at Mohammed's General Store from Johannesburg, usually ordered from colour catalogues. So PapaMac is our Father Christmas, in a dressing gown and carpet slippers, reading out the names on the gifts one by one around the Christmas tree. Us children are spoilt as usual, with roller skates and game compendiums, new clothes, Sunrise toffees and Cadbury chocolate. Even little Essie, who prefers the wrapping, is showered with a collection of new toys. Gaga says she'll buy the best frame she can find for the lemon painting.

My mother feigns absolute delight in her biscuit tin of treasures, though somehow they will never reach Rhodesia with the rest of our belongings. Martha cries when I give her the necklace with the royal feather and she promises to keep it forever. She folds me in her arms and squeezes all reproach right out of me.

Our lunch table, crisp with white linen, groans with the weight of roasts, of chickens and lamb and gammon and bowls of vegetables from PapaMac's garden. Though the lamb is too dry for teaspoons of blood tasting, even the Dad relaxes into the mood of happy reconciliation. After lunch he and Uncle George both have their noses in bottles and find everything funny. The Dad puts a record on the player and he dances circles on the green carpet with my mother. Uncle George stumbles an awkward wooden-leg waltz with Lally, occasionally winking over her shoulder at his wife, who sits quietly in one of Gaga's floral chairs, her balloon legs crossed in stolid resignation, her hands folded neatly on her lap as if she is waiting for a bus.

After a while the grown-ups retire to sleep off the bacchanalian feast while Thomas, Lally and I play outdoors on our roller skates.

Lally says she hates it when her father is drunk and dances with her. Drunk fathers do stupid things like stick their tongues in your ear, breathe whisky fumes into your face and press up against you so you can barely breathe. They seem funny and happy but they really aren't. They get into horrible moods sometimes and start throwing things around the house and banging their fists on tables. She is struggling to buckle her skates on and she suddenly starts crying. Thomas helps her with the straps and says that no one should cry on Christmas Day. I try to imagine things flying through the lemon lounge, little china cups edged with pink roses and Auntie Sylvia catching them before they break, her balloon legs tipped with high heels tripping through the air.

I know one thing to be true. Grown-ups can lose the bitterness and anger of the day in a glass or two of whisky. Thomas and I often go to bed sure that everything will be all right and find in the light of morning that it isn't true. The Dad's mellow moods are bottled in whisky or gin and bitters and we like him best after his evening 'snort'.

That night is the last time Lally stays with us in Little Ezulwini. She will go back to Jo'burg to stay with her father for the rest of the holidays. She is quieter than usual when we climb into our beds.

'I don't think I'll be coming back here much when you're gone,' she says when Thomas has turned off the light.

'You can still come and see Gaga and Papa,' says Thomas.

'It won't be the same.'

Lally sits up on her mattress, which is on the floor between our beds.

'Do you think you'll ever come back?'

'Dunno...' says Thomas.

'We'll come back,' I say, surprised at my own confidence.

Lally climbs onto my bed and slips between the sheets.

'If only you could stay...' She turns her face towards me. I reach under the covers for her hand.

That night, the night of our last Christmas in Swaziland, as I watch Lally close her eyes and fall asleep on my pillow, I send a prayer up into the thatch. I pray for something to happen to keep us all here. Anything. Though I know it will have to be something really big to make them change their minds.

VI

The Dad has planned everything. A double-storey house in Salisbury, a school for Thomas and me, and the trip that would take us up to

Beira where he'll fetch us in the jeep and take us the rest of the way. We are slowly packing up our lives into cardboard boxes. There is little left but the clothes we can fit into suitcases and a few odds and ends to keep us occupied until the end of January. The Dad's enthusiasm is contagious, and in the summer evenings our Mum sips her gin and bitters and dreams of her own home and garden. Thomas is wooed with the prospect of travelling on a train and a passenger boat across the ocean. We are in a space between, suffocating with the waiting. Expectancy and loss hang in the air and the sense of both hover in every room, in the smell of Jungle Oats porridge on the Arga stove and Lifebuoy soap on Martha's hands, wax polish on slasto floors, Yardley's lavender talc and mothballs in Gaga's bedroom, starched and ironed linen in the laundry. It splits us down the middle and the quiver of stowed tears is never far from inane laughter.

The chance of turning everything back is slim.

My grandmother spends more time lying in her darkened bedroom, curtains pulled closed to keep out the days. PapaMac wanders up and down his rows of vegetables, pressing the soil and picking out the weeds before they grow comfortable in the sunlight.

The measure of the passing days and nights is read in the face of the moon that waxes steadily from its shadowed sickle shape to its final luminance. The whole kingdom awaits the rising of that perfect silver orb. It promises the dance of Incwala, the first fruits, the coming of rain. The birth of change.

PART FIVE

The six days

It was early January and time for the days of Incwala. The six days of the Moon. And in six days our place in heaven faltered and on the seventh, for Thomas, God was dead.

The first day

The rites of the Great Incwala begin from the first day of the first full moon of the year. The king's appointed messengers have already been sent forth to gather secret herbs and waters from the rivers, the Great Usutu, the White Umbeluzi, the Black Umbeluzi, and then from the Indian Ocean across the Lubombo Mountains to the east of Mozambique.

The youngest of the chaste men stand before the king to sing his praises. The young warriors are sent out to a place called Egundweni, to cut and fetch the branches of the sacred lusekwane tree. They carry these back on their shoulders to Lobamba, the king's royal kraal, travelling over forty kilometres without rest. It is a test of their endurance, of their manhood. With these branches a bower is constructed in which the secret rituals take place.

For days the villages have been filled with the practice of ceremonial dances, the preparation of tribal dress exclusive to the seasonal rituals. Hair is combed and teased, often lathered with carbolic soap and bleached yellow. Anklets, bracelets and collars of blonde cow tails are washed and brushed. Belts and necklaces woven with tiny glass beads, sashes and cloaks of bright cotton fabric, aprons of leopard skin, ostrich plumes and birds' tail feathers for the hair — and that is just the men, the warriors of Incwala. The women are brightly dressed also, in scarlet, white and yellow. But it is the men who compete like peacocks at the time of the first moon.

By the time the full face of the moon peers down upon the kingdom from a velvet, star-studded sky, we have almost missed it. Martha comes to the rondavel to call us out in our pyjamas. It hangs just above the mountains, silver white. Tomorrow, she says, is the beginning of Big Incwala. Tomorrow we will wait at the gate.

This is to be my third time and I am a little less afraid, but still I hold fast onto Martha's hand when they come. Thomas scrambles up into the branches of the mimosa and gives us a running commentary like a radio announcer.

'Here they come, dressed in full costume of red and white cloaks and leopard skin,' Thomas shouts from his perch.

'Nkosi! Warriors of the Lion, marching up the hill and down towards the royal kraal of King Sobhuza!'

'Nkosi! Black mamba! Amaswati! Spears and shields and knobkerries rising and falling as they sing, an army of savage soldiers going to war!'

The voice of the Beast rises up from a distant rumble from the bottom of Malagwane road as the wave moves towards us, clouds of dust preceding them, knobkerrie tops and feathers. The chanting grows to a mesmerizing pitch as the men stamp over the rise, resplendent in full regalia, heads up high, eyes fixed on a destination only they can see. Leopard skin aprons swing from their hips, cowhide shields rise and fall with spears in even rhythm like the moon tide.

'Yebo! Inkosi!' Thomas whoops and shouts from the branches above us.

Through my feet I can feel the ground rumble.

This time there are warriors who salute us, men we vaguely recognize from the neighbouring location. Then comes Solomon, who lifts his shield towards Thomas and grins at Martha and me.

Thomas shouts: 'Yebo Solomon! Gijima wena! Hamba bo!'

He has dropped out of the tree and now begins his own rhythmic stamping on the ground, chanting and raising his boy fists in the air. This causes a few wry grins from the men, though most of them look ahead in proud disdain of this young white boy and his arrogance.

Amongst the final stragglers at the tail end are several men dressed in dusty baboon skins and seed beads, hair in red-mud coils. They are flicking black horse-tail whips. One of them nods in our direction and Martha grips my hand tightly. She inclines her head briefly in a moment of recognition and pulls me towards her.

'We must go back to the house,' she says.

'Who are those men with the whips?' I ask as we turn down the drive.

'Medicine men. Inyangas.'

'They're witch doctors,' says Thomas. 'They usually hide away because the government doesn't allow them and all their black magic here.'

'Do you know that one? The one who looked at us?' I ask.

'I don't know the witch doctors.'

'But you nodded at him.'

'I don't know him.'

'I'd like to be a warrior, marching to Incwala,' says Thomas.

'This you can never be, Master Thomas.'

'Yes, but sometimes I wish I was a real Swazi.'

Martha shakes her head.

'You be too white,' she says.

Back in the house, the air is filled with the sounds of 'The Student Prince' and Mario Lanza's tenor voice is competing with Essie's screaming in the kitchen. Gaga rocks back and forth on her floral rocking chair, staring out at the grey clouds gathering over the mountains, her fingers clicking needles in and out of her knitting with a momentum of their own.

I sit cross-legged on the carpet.

'Have the savages gone yet?'

'I saw witch doctors.'

'Have they all gone?'

'Yes.'

'Was Solomon with them?'

'He's a fine warrior.'

'He's my garden boy.'

'He's gone to the king's kraal for Incwala.'

'He should be planting the new roses.'

'Will there be a king in Rhodesia?'

'There's Queen Elizabeth in England, dear. That's all that matters. You're a little English girl, and don't you forget it.'

'Thomas says he wants to be a Swazi warrior.'

'Phha!' Gaga's fingers stop knitting.

'How can he possibly want to be like the natives?' she says.

The second day

The clouds billow over the valley in ominous assurance of a pending storm that never happens. The teasing of cloud-filled skies and even the low rumblings of thunder come to nothing and the hadedahs fly overhead, laughing at our thwarted expectations. My grandmother is hoping for a soaking rain for the planting of her roses. The ground remains hard and dry. Martha says only at Incwala's end will the heavens open and scatter the rains. So the days remain humid and the air thick with clammy summer heat.

Mum allows Thomas and me to walk up the hill if we promise to return before afternoon tea. She has her hands full with the packing of boxes and with Baby Essie, who is constantly fretting with the onset of new teeth. Essie's nanny, Salome, and Precious have gone home to practise their dancing for the coming festival.

The ground on the hill is still bare and parched black from the fire. With so little rain there isn't much sign of new growth and the exposed rocks stand out like dry scabs on naked stubble. It isn't long before our legs are covered in soot.

The fire has uncovered a multitude of objects rusted with time and blackened with fire; tinned-fruit cans, a bicycle rim, an old milk urn, a cigarette tin, bits and pieces of an old car engine, remnants of untold stories. Shrubs and trees are scorched and stripped of their mortal greenery like forlorn skeletons. There are real skeletons too, a rock hare, a mongoose and the skull of a baby baboon, the ones that couldn't escape the ravages of an untimely cremation. We find a small tortoise shell empty of its former inhabitant. We collect all our findings and place them in a heap like a fond memorial to dead relatives, the forgotten evidence of another life, a grave of rusted metal and brittle bones. We gather scorched granite and agate stones and bury a history under them in a mound as big as a termite nest. This is what we'll leave behind us, says Thomas, after four years in the kingdom of Swaziland.

He has scooped up some soot from the ground and he spits into the palm of his hand. He rubs it on his face. I squeal with delight.

We both rub the black soot-ash into our skin, laughing and giggling at our transformation. Thomas forages around for two sticks to serve as knobkerries and we stamp around our burial mound, two crazed siblings whooping and yelling.

Later, all our energy spent, we sit on the flat rock overlooking the valley of Ezulwini.

'We must promise to come back.' Thomas's words are uttered earnestly from a pink mouth in a pitch-black face, the whites of his eyes pearl blue.

We seal our promise in a sooty handshake. Then Thomas lies back on his elbows and smokes a Peter Stuyvesant stompie.

When we return our mother says, 'You look like Poorwhites!' and orders a painful scrubbing from Martha with soap, Dettol and a nailbrush before she allows us back into the house.

We are sitting at the kitchen table, shining neon pink and burning clean, and dunking Marie biscuits in our tea when we hear a commotion coming from the lounge. Above the thumping and crashing sounds our mother's voice is rising taut as fence wire, high and hysterical, an alarming pitch the colour of bitter green... a parroting squawk more unlike my mother's quiet reserve than you could imagine.

My brother and I leap to our feet and race in the direction of this strangely aberrant noise. We find her in the lounge, holding a broom aloft and smacking the lounge ceiling, half crazed. The Dad is just standing there watching her, a wide grin written in the creases of his face.

'This is quite the most pathetic thing!' he says.

'It has to go! For God's sake give me a hand!' She shrieks again as an urgent flutter of wings swoops over her head.

'It's just a sparrow. Why are you getting all hot under the collar?'

'Thomas, get some dishcloths from the kitchen!' squawks this mad, bad mother.

My brother doesn't stop to ask questions, but dashes back to the kitchen as if he has caught the urgency that the Dad and I do not understand.

The bird is huddled in the corner of the room, perched on the maroon velvet pelmet. Its tiny chest moves up and down with its breathing, or is it his frantically beating heart? The fragile creature is stricken with fear. My mother is a witch with a broomstick and there is murder in her eyes. There is no question in my mind which one of them is the victim.

'Stoppit! Stoppit!' I scream.

My screams tear at my throat. I grab onto her skirt. She lets the broom fall and gapes at me, anguish ridden, not comprehending.

The Dad pushes me violently from behind.

'Hey! You…!'

I sprawl headlong and spread-eagled at her feet. My mother slumps to the floor beside me and cradles her face in her hands. And while the Dad looks on in uncertain confusion, Thomas runs to the windows and opens them wide, then he whirls the cloths round in the air, spinning a dervish dance on the carpet, like he's done this all before; he's an aeroplane with dishcloth propellers rushing towards the open windows as if he is about to launch himself into the air outside. The sparrow flutters once or twice in anxious hesitation, then flies out across the terraced lawn and into the safety of the wide blue sky.

The way her shoulders are shaking, I think my mother will never stop crying, but when she lifts her face she's laughing so hard her eyes are wet with tears.

'It's okay. It's gone,' says Thomas.

'Christ's sake, you're all bloody barmy!' the Dad says as he turns and walks out the room.

'Don't tell Gaga, Jilly, Thomas. Don't tell her about the bird.'

But our grandmother has found the sparrow feathers, soft, downy and speckled brown, on the carpet after dinner. She scoops them up in her hand and scatters them outside. We watch her in expectation of a torrid reaction, but she says nothing. She retires to her bedroom early without a mention of the bird. Thomas says that maybe sparrows don't count; it is usually black birds that bring the curse. Mum looks at us like she is the teacher and we are her lost boys, and she casts a fickle bridge of shallow laughter over our fear.

'Superstitious nonsense!' she says.

The third day

On the third day of the Great Incwala, the king's army has gathered in Lobamba, thousands upon thousands of brightly clad warriors from the valleys and the mountains of Swaziland. As dusk draws a deepening hue on the wide dome of sky, the drumming begins and the voices rise in sibilant sound like the rushing and sighing of the sea.

Above the royal stage the hardly waning moon is a virgin face, hallowed in a silver veil, haloed.

A rumble of hooves scatters clouds of dust-like smoke upwards into the fading light as the ox stumbles forth. He is a heaving monolith, a pitch-black shadow beast, his power restrained only by his confusion. A throng of unflinching warriors drives him forward into the bower of lusekwane branches. He strains violently against his captors as they bear him down, and his breathing comes out quick and sharp for the size of him. The hands of the royal sangomas are shining wet with bitter herbs, sour oils that reach into the nostrils and sting the eyes like pepper, muti for the ritual cleansing. When the beast emerges from the bower, his eyes are red wild, his great chest is heaving. He is bewildered, uncertain. With what he perhaps knows is his final defence, he bellows and lunges towards the surging mass of young men. But the circle closes in now, thrusting, pressing, and the ox spins around and stumbles. From his belly like a hollow cowhide drum, a terrible groan rolls deep as night, dark and coarse and guttural. In the rising raw sanguine dust the black bodies of the men push and swell together. Behind them the still, cool sky is a deep cerulean blue.

In one voice they surge inward.

This is when they rush the beast, encircle it, shoving forward, tightly trapping it with their bodies. They pummel it with their fists, hitting and beating the rank sweating hide, a hundred closed hands drumming, flesh on flesh, until he finally submits, rolling over onto his back, bruised and succumbing to exhaustion. His final resistance breathes out of his quivering nostrils, an involuntary shudder runs through his limbs, a tremor rippling like water across the skin. They heave the inert animal above their heads with the song of the brave, the strong men, no longer boys. They will carry the beast back to the bower where the ox is ritually slaughtered, knife to flesh, flesh to bone, as he slowly expires, giving in to the final sacrifice.

Now the king, Ngwenyama, the lion, enters the bower. He is carefully stripped naked of all his clothing and lifted onto the back of the slaughtered beast.

His body is washed tenderly with Sidwasho, the sacred waters from the great rivers and the sea, combined with the pungent mixture of crushed herbs. This is the mystical rite. The king is thus cleansed and purified and the virility of the black ox enters him, for he and his land are inextricably one and it is in this manner that the land is assured of its fertility for the coming year and the kingdom is restored once again.

On the night of the third day, two white children in flannel pyjamas leave their beds and walk barefoot over the stone path and around the side of the house, taking care not to make a sound. By the light of moonshine they run down the dew-damp terraced lawns, through the corridors between the young pines – saplings, not yet trees. The soft needles beneath their feet exude a fine balsamic tang they can almost taste as they run. Beyond the pinewood, the boy picks his way carefully over the scrubby mounds of grass and prickly aloes, stepping on the smooth mounds of granite rock, and the girl follows the invisible hieroglyphs of his footprints. They know the path so well they could run it in their sleep. They reach the edge of the jagged rocks where the ground plunges downwards some hundreds of feet to the new road they are making below. Here they sit on a rock, not yet cold after the day's heat, breathing in the pungent smells of coarse grass and sappy succulents, so much sharper under a dark sky.

The sky itself is a glass dome, window to a heaven that is everywhere and nowhere, here and far away. There is an immortal presence in the immutable weight of mountains that wait and watch, deep in ancient knowing, lodged in a history before time. Silence is the gratefulness of a mother's upturned hands, the generous space that holds the shape of sounds. Now it is only the far-off drumming beating steadily from the heart of the valley below that measures the quiet against itself. It murmurs secrets from the royal kraal, from the ground that trembles under the feet of so many, where the blood of the black ox spills on the trampled earth of the bower because death must come for new life to begin. Like a lamb's blood, a man hung on a cross, a promise like a scarlet thread tied at a window.

Ethereal mists rise like fine breathing above the fir trees and the gum forests on the mountain slopes. The boy takes a filter cigarette and a box of Lion matches from his pyjama pocket. He lights it and inhales the smoke like a seasoned veteran. The girl watches the cirrus clouds escape from his mouth and nose, drift to disperse into nothingness in the air.

From the mountains behind they hear a sound like the high rasping call of a leopard. Just the one call, so they can't be sure. But in their minds she is there, wandering the rocky escarpment above the blackened grass, watching the valley, surveying the kingdom like the god Osiris, the watcher, judge of the souls of men. She is everything that is beautiful and powerful, everything savage and cruel. The boy can hardly distinguish the love from the fear she stirs in him. For him she is dream-tangible, desire realized, a god-like creature so much more than himself and all he believes. She is something that he recognises but yet eludes him. He knows. But he does not know what he knows.

They do not speak at all.

The silence that holds the occasional night sounds is too immense to break. The girl watches the boy's face, profiled against the moon-bright sky. With her eyes she traces the straight nose, the pouting lips, the heavy curls that fall about the wide forehead. She waits for him to speak. She has always waited for him.

The boy draws in a shuddering breath and sighs. She thinks he might say something then, but whatever it is, it remains just that, something he might have said, for that is when they hear the scream, that bitter-sharp, that harsh and strangling sound that could almost be animal, but you know is human. It is the excruciating human cry of pain too much, too much to bear. It has come from behind them, from the direction of the house, ripping like torn silk through the cool quiet.

The girl grabs the boy's arm. Quickly, the boy says.

They run back over the rocks, tripping and tearing over the scrub and slashing through the whipping needles of the pine branches, over the cool wet grass and up towards the house. It isn't the sound of their running that is loud. It's their breathing. She hears a strange whimpering, surprised that it comes from her because it is an alien sound she does not recognise. A strangling fist of panic has lodged itself in her throat.

They slow down as they pass the house. The boy grabs hold of her hand. The dampness of the grass has crept up her pyjama legs and she shivers. But it isn't just the cold, it is the image of a leopard, crouching in the shadows of a garden in the night. She can see her everywhere, under the azalea shrubs, leaning against the wall by the tap, lying motionless beneath the hydrangeas, sprawled across the lower branch of a jacaranda. She wants to shut her eyes and run blind. Is it cruelty that burns from orbs of marbled fire? Flesh torn from flesh in a garden ripe with the sweet scent of flowers? She wishes that someone would pick her up and carry her away, above the long shadows on the lawn, over the flowerbeds and the slasto and the stones that bite your feet, someone strong enough to save her from the wildness of this place, this heaven where the leopards live.

Faint moonbeams on a dark stair... air stirred and shaken... the scream they can no longer hear follows them like grasping fingers as they run. They are the Listeners, straining to hear something else past the stillness. But the house is asleep, still, undisturbed under its hood of thatch; the windows stare blankly at them with dark eyes reflecting the many faces of a quite benevolent moon. No one stirs as they slip round the back and across the path towards the rondavel.

They stand breathless in the quiet of their room and listen. Even the distant drumming, the beetle song, the bullfrogs, croaking has stopped as if in humble veneration, a moment's modest empathy.

The room is just as they'd left it, rumpled beds, scattered books, a half empty glass of milk on the table, the quiet radio grinning on the floor, objects benign and unchanged. The sameness of everything mocks them, the way that objects look at you when they are pretending nothing's happened.

But it wasn't nothing. They know that much.

The fourth day

The first light of dawn washed a muted azure haze above the mountains and the sun daubed the clouds cerise before it rose. That was how Gaga saw it from her bedroom window on the fourth day.

On the fourth day the king walks like Moses through the sea of warriors who crouch low on the dusty ground, an ocean of heads bowed in submission to the Great Ngwenyama, the Lion.

He is anointed with black medicine, herbs and green grass, wearing a headdress of long black ostrich plumes and a belt of silver monkey skins. Now the queen mother, who is called Ndlovukazi, leads the royal women in song. A mesmerizing dance begins, the gentle swaying of hips and breasts, then the low hum of the voices of men through the descent. The singing swells and fills the valley with its sound.

In the centre the king begins the dance of Incwala, and the warriors rise up with shields lifted high, their bare feet stamping the ground in metronomic rhythm so that the royal kraal trembles with the stamping and drumming and the joyful ululation.

And tonight the king will sleep alone with the first wife, the wife of his first ritual marriage. That is the tradition.

The urgent banging on the kitchen door is rude and intrusive at this hour of the day, the old house drowsy still with sleep. But there it comes again, loud and insistent. When Gaga opens the door and sees him standing there, for a second she doesn't know him. For a second he is the savage native who visits her dreams, the apparition of black Africa she fears the most. His hair is teased back and garnished with bird feathers. He wears a brilliant scarlet cloth knotted on the shoulder, and several long strands of beads wound about his neck and torso, anklets and bracelets of soft blonde cow tails.

'Please,' he is saying, 'please, Ma'am. No time now. Please to call the baas to come now.'

'Solomon? Why aren't you dressed properly?'

'I am sorry for this. Please, Ma'am. Maningi trouble, Ma'am.'

'What trouble, Solomon? You bring trouble to my house this early?'

'Problem up there at the compound, Ma'am.' He is wringing his hands and nodding in agitation for the time the old woman is wasting.

She notices for the first time the leopard skin worn like an apron at his waist. She thinks for a moment it is quite beautiful with the black rosettes on the gold. Then she dismisses the notion and backs into the kitchen.

'I'll call my husband,' she says.

The sun has not yet risen above the mountains when PapaMac marches up to the compound in his dressing gown and carpet slippers. He has noted the urgency in Solomon's voice at once. He can hear Martha's sobbing before he reaches her door, which is open and badly in need of a new coat of paint, a couple of screws in a hinge and a new lock.

The room is dimly lit with the light of a single candle, so it takes his eyes a while to adjust, to find out the focus of this trouble. On Martha's iron bed, raised up on bricks, is a girl not much older than eighteen. Despite all the snivelling and sobbing that comes from the mother, the girl appears to be sleeping. Then Solomon reaches forward and pulls back the blankets. The old man feels the familiar contraction of a fist around his heart. This is a different story altogether. The lower half of the white sheet beneath the girl's folded legs and bare buttocks is soaked in blood. He takes a step forward and looks at the child's face again, and he notices the strange pallor. He doesn't wait for questions and answers. There is no time for splitting hairs over who is to blame and why. He turns away.

PapaMac is shuffling down to the house as fast as he can with the shortness of breath, a constricted chest and carpet slippers. The doctor could take too long. Bryan must take the girl in the Jeep to Mbabane hospital. No time. Enough wasted already. He is convinced it's probably too late. PapaMac musters what strength he can and assumes his quiet authority.

'You take her up to Mbabane hospital to the native emergency as quickly as you can. And take Martha with you. We'll need extra blankets. Hurry it up, that girl's about to bleed to death. Get Solomon to help you carry her.'

Folded blankets are pushed into the Jeep and the door slams behind its reluctant driver. It revs up a storm of loose gravel on the drive as it turns sharply out of the gate.

That is when Thomas and I wake, with the harsh grating of gears and the gravel stones flying from the Jeep's tyres. I still have no idea that Rahab has returned, or that it was she who was there at the location at the time of the fire, with Thomas. But the memory of a scream heard in the night is with me when I wake up, like a cold hard fact in an unfinished story.

By the time Thomas and I wander into the kitchen that morning, PapaMac is lying down in his bedroom, waiting for his pills to bring some calm to his agitated heart. Gaga and Mum are drinking tea in the stark white light of the kitchen, unable to face the stack of dishes and pots that litter the sideboard and the sink, weak at the thought of dirty clothes and starching, the bleaching and the ironing that lie in untidy heaps on the laundry floor. Now with Martha gone for the day, and the maids dancing in the valley, there'll be no help at all. No servers. Servantless.

'That bird...' says my grandmother.

'It was only a sparrow.'

'Nevertheless...'

'Do you think it was a miscarriage?' my mother says. She is looking out the kitchen window at nothing in particular, one hand cupping her chin and the other holding her cup in the air like an offering.

'Something. Perhaps a baby, if that's what it was.'

'Perhaps the girl. They might not have made it in time.'

They tell us that Martha and the Dad have driven to the hospital in Mbabane.

There was an accident, they say, up at the compound.

'What girl?' Thomas asks.

'I think it was Martha's daughter, the one that was here before. I didn't even know she had come back,' our Mum says.

'Is it Rahab?' I ask.

'What kind of a name is that?' says Gaga.

'She's been sick for a long time.'

'What accident?' asks Thomas, warily.

'We're not sure...' my mother shrugs. I can see that Thomas wants to say more, but he bites back the words. We shouldn't have been out in the middle of the night. We shouldn't have heard the scream. It seems that no one else had.

'Is she going to die?'

'I don't think so, Jilly.'

'Someone is,' says Gaga.

We do not know it but Solomon has crept away as the dawn inched slowly across the sky, pulling behind it a shy and reluctant sun from behind the mountain, the valley remaining dark with shadow. Taking a garden spade and an old hessian coalbag, he runs along the footpath from the vegetable garden and up the scorched hill. Then he zig-zags across the burnt scrub, leaping from rock to ground, over the prickly stubble.

His eyes scan the ground for a fresh mound of earth, some sort of disturbance. Finding a newly built mound of stones, he tears away at it only to discover a curious collection of charred bones and metal rubbish. He moves further up the hill, running in desperate circles round blackened trees and singed shrubs, until he reaches the top. From there he can see the sudden dip into the valley and where the rocky escarpment of the mountain begins. He can see the line where the fire had burnt a jagged edge up the mountain slope and stopped suddenly.

Then his eyes are startled by something brilliant white, caught in the first rays of the morning sun. He clambers down the rugged rocks, and across the black, tearing through acacia thorn. It takes him a while to cross the valley dip, this side of the farm compound where the undergrowth is thick and untouched by fire or men. He scrambles up, half climbing up rockbeds, pulling at virgin wattle saplings, anything that he can grab onto to hoist him upwards.

There was no grave, just a shallow donga, and a sheet that lay crumpled, bare and bloody like a gaping mouth. The baby was gone. He stood staring at it in disbelief. Could only be an animal, he thought, a hyena, a jackal, even a leopard.

He wonders whether he should turn back. Without the baby there would be less trouble. The white people would ask fewer questions. They would soon forget about a black baby lost on the mountain. His mind turned somersaults: these questions, those excuses, a lie here, a story there, but none of it would seem plausible. What if they blamed him? No one had seen the inyanga, maybe they'd blame him for taking the child? He began to run, scrambling desperately, steeply, upwards, through grass gold and waist high, over the rocks. He held the spade aloft. Now he was yelling, shouting, screaming. The beast would know that this was Solomon the warrior, flying up the slope, his scarlet cloth whipping behind him.

Solomon found the infant lying face down in the fork of a white thorn acacia. It was not difficult, as there were few trees at the base of the incline, and her small body had not been taken up much higher than the first few branches. The child's body was intact. There were two neat puncture marks on the neck whereby she'd been carried the distance from the sheet in the donga to the tree. There was no sign of the leopard.

Solomon had returned to the house by the time the Dad came back from Mbabane late that morning with Martha sitting stony-still in the back seat. A police van had followed the jeep and parked up at the compound. Two black policemen searched the compound while the white officers came down to the house to ask questions. Thomas and I sit on the back lawn while they drink tea and speak to the grown-ups. The sunlight is now starkly bright, the day indecently perfect.

I want to cry for Rahab. I am sure she is dead. Was it the leopard? Had Shaba come in the night and found her washing at the compound tap? Had she crept up on her and surprised her, and in one leap ripped into her flesh with terrible teeth? I am seven years old, almost eight and a child grown up with fairy tales of terrors far worse than this. One of the policemen walks stiffly up the path and stands in front of Thomas and me, so that his shadow casts an elongated cartoon copy of him on the grass.

He wants to know about Rahab. How long has she been here?

Have we spoken to her? Do we know anything about a baby? What did they tell us? Thomas and I look at him dumbfounded. Why is he asking? We know little more than nothing. There is no baby, we said. Only Baby Elizabeth.

'And the girl they call Rahab?'

Thomas shrugs.

'Is she dead?' I say and the words in my throat become tears.

The policeman shrugs.

We hear the sound of agitated voices coming from the compound. Martha is wailing above the sharp voices of men.

The policeman walks briskly up the path towards the commotion. Thomas and I follow him. We stand behind the lantana bushes so the grown-ups won't send us away.

Solomon, still dressed like a Swazi warrior, is streaked with sweat and black soot. His eyes are wide and wild, his breathing is shallow and quick, like a bird caught and cornered in a room. He is shouting at Martha, incomprehensible words bumping and clicking together on a thread. Martha's face is swollen, her eyes fierce as she rattles back at the warrior. All this anger is scarlet red. The whole world seems washed with it. Or perhaps it is just here where the black people live, the sky is still a clean bright blue, and the new chickens are grumbling about a late breakfast. Solomon holds up a hessian bag. It sways with the weight of what it contains.

'You want your baby?' he shouts in English.

Martha wails, lashing out at him. She has turned into a cat, hissing and snarling. One of the black policemen grabs at her arms and pulls her back. Her mouth is open wide and pink like a wound, her teeth salt washed and so white I cannot look at her any more. She is not my nanny. This is a strange black woman I do not know. The way she screams like that, raw and wild, animal, it is a savage rage that makes my stomach sick with fear and I turn and run towards the house.

They take them both away in the back of the van, Martha and Solomon. They put the hessian bag in the front between the two white officers like a parcel from the post office, and drive away, up the circular drive and out the whitewashed gates, leaving a quiet finality behind them in the settling dust.

Later that day the Dad drives to the Mbabane police station, and returns a few hours later, his mood eased with Tavern beer, his words slow and self-assured.

So by late afternoon we know. Not about Martha's careful plan to hide the shame, or the breech birth that nearly killed Rahab. He spares us those details. But he tells us, Thomas and me, about a witchdoctor who sneaked into the khaya in the dark middle-of-the-night. He describes it as a merciless attack on the girl, cutting at the tender flesh between her legs, and stealing the baby from her, wrapping it in bloodied sheets, leaving the girl-mother to bleed to death in her bed. Witches steal children for muti. Then he tells us about the leopard. My stepfather has spared us nothing. He makes a meal of the telling of it, served up with all the gruesome details, a macabre feast he will watch us swallow – and we do.

We sit there appalled and listening so intently, we leave nothing untouched, not one thing spilt; we must have it all, digesting the terrible images so that we will remember them later in cruel detail. The leopard killed her, he says, taking her from the sheet (red-stained and wet with her mother's blood) from a shallow donga on the hill, where the inyanga had left her. Who followed the moon moth? Careless witch, care-less. The leopard broke her tiny neck, he says, fragile, snap... like a dry twig, and carried her in her mouth, her small head grasped firmly in those massive jaws, and teeth this long and tearing sharp. The leopard carried her, so light was she, to the foot of the granite escarpment, where she secured the tiny infant corpse in the forked branches of a thorn tree, white thorns like fangs, needle sharp. Then she would have licked her clean, the dried and muddy streaks of afterbirth, with her rough tongue, the way that leopards do before they eat their prey, before the belly is ripped open, gaping, like the dark wet insides of the pomegranate fruit. Pomegranate fruit, ripe and scarlet inside like a secret. Terrible secret.

The Dad sits back in his chair, sucking in the blue smoke from another cigarette, washing back another mouthful of beer. So, he says, if Solomon hadn't rushed down the hill yelling blue murder like that, there would have been nothing left of that little black bastard to find. And there's no sense in looking for the inyanga now; they are sly and slippery people, the Dad says. Witches. He'll have disappeared into the shadows by now, and never found. That's what they're like, he says.

'And the leopard?' Thomas asks, his voice small, but strangely piqued with antipathy.

'Ah,' says the Dad, 'the leopard.'

But he leaves Thomas's question to hang in the uncertainness he dreads.

The Dad's story is repeated and examined and spilt out in a river of unstoppable hysteria. The house is filled with the horror of it.

So the leopard is the perpetrator. The savage intent of this most awful thing is hers alone. The child has died of suffocation and a broken neck. The way she was found, in the fork of the tree, and the two clean and deep incisions are sufficient evidence. She is judged and found guilty.

But it is a merciful end with little struggle and suffering is not prolonged.

The fifth day

Day five of Incwala is a day of rest and quiet contemplation. No work is done on the fifth day.

Ezulwini is shrouded in the shadow of heavy cloud and mist that settles over the valley and hides the mountains from us. It is fitting weather for the sombre mood that lies heavily upon all of us this day, the fifth day of Incwala. Gaga and our Mum busy themselves with housework most of the day, cleaning and scrubbing with the sharp smells of bleach and ammonia as if they could wash the stains of yesterday away like filthy grime. As if in the neatness of folded clothes and dusted furniture they could return to the comfort of forgetting, of not knowing. After all, Gaga said, all this native trouble has nothing to do with us.

The Dad has gone off somewhere in his jeep, and Papa lies in bed, unwilling to test the strain of his uncertain heart. My brother and I spend most of the day in the pages of cheap comics, moving in lizard time and trying to forget. The morbid quietness numbs us, keeps us from each other.

In the afternoon I creep into the house and stand over Essie's cot where she is closeted in a warm deep sleep. Beneath long blonde lashes, her cheeks are flushed rose pink. In the humidity of the afternoon, fine strands of hair have stuck to her forehead. I lean over and smell that familiar sweet, that milky breath. The way she lay there wrapped in flannel cotton, pink and perfect, untouched, never harmed, I feel a breathless relief. I don't want to remember the other baby. The room is painted a pale blue, and her little things smile from the walls and shelves. Contented clowns and bears and plastic dolls stare at the window. The whole room is filled with pastel-coloured promises.

I think of all the stories she'll come to know, and the nursery rhymes she'll learn, of Rumpelstiltskin, and the badness of wolves, of babies and cradles falling from trees. I don't want to remember the other baby at all.

As I turn towards the passage I hear my mother's voice, low and insistent.

'You can't tell Thomas. Just do it quietly. He doesn't have to know.'

'Thomas knows where the leopard lair is. That's where he was the day of the fire. He was looking for the damn thing, I'm bloody sure of it.' The Dad's voice.

'You'll take some trackers with you? Someone that knows the mountain?'

'Of course we'll take some boys with us. But it would be that much easier if we had some idea of her exact location.'

'Not Thomas,' my mother says vehemently.

'For God's sake, when are you going to let the boy grow up?'

Her voice turns away and I don't catch what she is saying.

'Well, it may take the whole night. It won't be much of a picnic,' he says.

'Much of a picnic? You're going to shoot it, Bryan, not invite it to tea.'

'That's if it doesn't get me first.'

Perhaps it is in that last sentence. Perhaps it is the need to end the horror of it all. Or maybe, in the reckoning of a manipulative child, I see the opportunity of turning back the painful inevitability of leaving. I'm not sure what is running through my mind when I step into the passage and see him standing there.

'I know where the leopard is,' I say.

Once spoken the words cannot be taken back. At least Thomas doesn't know I've told.

Thomas and I have our supper in the kitchen that night. We pick at our food with little interest, both overcome with an exhaustion we can't explain. Our mother is overly attentive, wrapping us in tenderness like a soothing balm. Only her eyes, darting towards the darkness behind the kitchen window, betray the nervousness I know she is trying to hide.

Thomas lets me lie with him in his own bed. He holds onto me while I shiver under the blankets. Eventually I succumb to the numb dreams of senseless times and illogical places, the safety of sleep. I feel Thomas's body jolt suddenly, and my mind returns with the remembering.

Thomas sits up and looks at the door.

'What?' I ask and my stomach twists. If they have brought him back from the mountain, I don't want to see. They will tell us about it in the morning, that it was an accident, that we'll be unpacking all the boxes now, that there is no point in going away now.

Thomas grabs his dressing gown and puts it on as he runs to the door.

I am crying.

'Stop blubbing and you can come with me.'

'I'm scared,' I say, but I follow him out anyway, because the prospect of being alone and not knowing is worse.

We hear their voices as we run across the slasto path towards the kitchen and then past the hydrangeas towards the front of the house.

The Dad is standing on the gravel drive, a rifle held loosely at his side. He is strangely red in the light of the porch, and his white grin beneath his moustache is incongruously bright. Our mother stands in the open doorway, a frozen statue wrapped in a sugar pink nightgown. She holds her fist up to her mouth and she is crying. I run to her and bury my face in the softness of the silk that covers her.

Thomas stands on the step, uncertain.

'Take the gun, my boy,' the Dad says, and I turn round to see Thomas staring at him, his face stony white.

'This is the gun of a hunter. Come on, take it.' He moves forward into the light. It is only then that I see the redness is blood, streaked down from his forehead and soaked into his shirt and down his pants to his boots. So much blood means death, I'm sure, and I expect him to fall down. Thomas moves forward a step and hesitates.

'The leopard's dead,' the Dad says. Just like that.

For a moment, a fraction, the cricket's song was the only sound there was.

Then Thomas's scream, strangled and raw, the sort of sound that you can feel grinding stones in your belly, that twists you inside out and leaves you trembling.

Then Thomas is running towards him. He throws himself at him, hitting his blood-soaked chest with small tight fists of rage.

He is screaming, 'It wasn't her fault! You bloody killed her! And it wasn't her fault!'

He is like a wild creature, a cornered cat crazed with terror. The Dad grips his flailing arms. A sharp blow with the full force of his open hand sends Thomas reeling to the ground where he crumples like a suddenly unstrung puppet and the screaming stops.

Mum lifts him up, gently boy, gently, and leads him like a baby back to the rondavel.

I stand at the bathroom door and watch her wash Thomas in the insect bath. His body is limp as she holds his hands and face over the bath and he watches the blood of the leopard disappear from him.

I still remember the naked light bulb that swayed above the bath and shone in my mother's hair, her hands rubbing the blood from Thomas's hair and the pinkness of the water that took it away.

I cannot sleep the whole night, though I know that the worst of my life must be over. I cannot stop thinking how wrong I was, how stupid to think he'd never come back. I measure my guilt in conspiring to force the end of this story myself. I must own it, wrap it up and hide it away.

I wonder whom I feel sorry for the most. My brother who lies deathly pale and unmoving beside me in the dark, the leopard whom we named and cast as our heroine and protagonist in the story of our young lives, or Rahab and a dead baby we had never known.

For Thomas there is no doubt.

'I'll hate him forever,' he whispers suddenly and vehemently in the dark.

The sixth day

In the morning a soft rain falls, drifting over the surprised kikuyu grass and soaking the dust from the leaves. The smell of it is mint fresh and familiar. The eaves drip, the thatch swells, and the swallows and the rollers dip and dive through the soft shower like a holiday.

When the rain stops, a mist rises from the cooling earth.

The sixth day, the last day of Incwala, a huge bonfire is lit. The king's bedding and clothing and various implements from the previous year and the remains of the slaughtered ox are burnt on the fire. For the kingdom it is a day of rejoicing, of glad song and festive celebration, the beginning of a new and fruitful year. Prayers have been offered to the gods for abundant rains. Every year, almost without fail, the rain comes on the last days of Incwala.

This morning they have brought Shaba's body down from the mountain. They lay her out on the porch, the Dad's trophy. Her mouth is slightly open, the size of her teeth alarmingly large. Her eyes are like frosted glass stained straw yellow, and already edged with flies. I wish my brother could see the size of her paws.

But Thomas doesn't want to see her.

This is the day the leopard has fallen, and God is dead.

PART SIX

The end

I am lying in a deep bath, in water so hot it scalds the skin red. I shift my knees and slip my head under, then my face, until warm nothingness is all there is, with only the muffled drumming of my own heart. Today I called home from the hotel foyer in Mbabane. My oldest daughter's voice pulled me into the kitchen hall at home, her anxious face reflected in the mirror above the phone, melting in the relief of knowing of my safe return. Then the youngest, animated with her own news and reproachfully reminding me of the snatches of their lives I'd missed. And my husband, Come home soon. We miss you, you've no idea…

How easily I have shed the roles of mother-wife in the last five weeks. In the bathroom mirror I surprised the woman that stared back at me, gaunt and weathered after weeeks of bundu life. Living on the edge of the wilderness, following the heartbeat of an ancient pard, I have found inside me an infinite space. I have seen myself through the eyes of the Watcher.

Last night I told them about Rahab and the baby. Sitting there in the comforting glow of the campfire, the words I spoke drifted up through the smoke but they were not enough to do justice to the horror of it. I am not a storyteller like Thomas.

It was years later that Thomas and I heard the whole story. My mother had known it all along, she had kept it buried along with the other things she had no wish to remember.

I have traced the details in my mind, watched it in replay, so that none of it escapes me. I have lived this dream in a black mother's skin.

Rahab's scream had torn a hole in the stillness of the third night, the night of the black ox. Only for a second before it was snuffed out in the grubby ticking of a feather pillow.

The baby girl, not much bigger than a small plucked chicken, was not a normal birth; she had to be turned in the womb like the farmers do sometimes in lamb birthing. The inyanga, a witch doctor of corruptible reputation, paid for mischief but unsure of midwifery, had torn the child too early from her mother's womb. He wrapped it in a blood-soaked sheet at the foot of the iron bed that stood high off the floor on bricks because of the Tokoloshe.

Afterwards, he wiped his bloody hands on a clean tea towel.

Martha sat askew on the bedside, her eyes fixed on a stain on the magazine-page wallpaper above Rahab's head. Behind her, smart Sunday clothes hung in smiling colours on wire hangers on the wall, decent church-going witnesses. Yawning biscuit tins were piled haphazardly on the pine shelf. The room was in unfamiliar disarray.

Hallowed-be-Thy-name-Thy-kingdom-come… and the infant beat her fists against the wrapping sheet, grabbing for her first breath somewhere beneath the folds. But Martha looked down at her daughter's face, wiping it gently with a damp cloth. For her, only the two of them existed in the dimly lit room. She smiled at Rahab. Thula'sana, thula, she whispered to the girl, though she slept still in a stone dream. The air in the small room was clammy with sweat, with hot breath, and thick with the smell of candle wax, raw blood, animal-like. In the valley of darkness… No sound now but whispering prayers like leaves taken by the wind. …I will fear no evil.

The inyanga rose to his feet, the tails of dead wild cats swaying loosely from his shoulders. He was impatient. He flicked the horse tail whip above the girl's limp body, and threw out empty murmurings, witches' spells, a glib panacea. He was in a hurry. Around his ankles tiny seed-filled cocoons rattled as he moved towards the wide-girthed woman. Martha reached into her bosom and pulled out a handkerchief of folded pound notes. Still she would not let her eyes betray her by looking at the end of the bed and her lips moved with the mechanical words of a prayer she knew so well the sense of it escaped her.

He tucked the notes under his apron, a grey and tatty baboon skin, reached out and grabbed the discarded bundle under his arm like a bag of dirty laundry, tossed the brick aside with his foot and then he disappeared out the blistered green door into the night.

II

I suppose that was the night this story really began, though the white people slept soundly in their big white house surrounded by their fine tea sets and fresh clean linen, floral couches, French polished wood and velvet curtains with gold brocade and thick silk carpets from China. They slept through it all without blame, under a porcelain moon. Why should there be blame? After all, their trouble is their own, their ways so separate, and as such this was an irrelevance we could well do without.

Only in the startling light of the new day, the fourth day, it became real.

There was no inquest. No retribution.

Martha was never prosecuted, though the madness of the wild dog that was visited upon her never really left. I saw her only once after the fourth day. She held me in the folds of her apron and reminded me to pray. It would save me from the darkness, she said. But my heart had already grown distant from her; it was time to shake off that intimate bonding with black mothers, the identity that white children inherit from the laps of their nannies. They were different from us, and it was time for me to grow up.

I sometimes wonder if Solomon had not returned before dawn to keep his promise to plant my grandmother's roses in the front garden, if Martha hadn't retracted under the weight of religious conscience, if Rahab had not begun haemorrhaging a few hours after the birth… we might never have known. They would never have found the child and all the secrets would have remained where they were, like dormant seeds with no water to make them grow.

There would have been no story. Just the coming and going of a typical white family who once lived in a small country in Africa and left hardly a trace behind them.

Martha had told Solomon she'd changed her mind. She didn't want the baby to be lying somewhere on the hill in a shallow grave. She wanted the priest to pray over the baby. She wanted to bury her first grandchild in the graveyard beside the African Native Church of England. She held no illusions of heaven for herself. Not now. How could God forgive such things? He would never condone the conspiracy, the black magic and trickery of witches. She begged Solomon that morning to find the child, to find the newly dug grave on the hill where the inyanga had buried it.

Solomon said later that Martha was crazy with the native madness. You could see the madness of the wild dog in her eyes, he said. I don't know whether she finally buried her grandchild or where.

I told Winston and the others:

'Rahab was to marry the Induna's first son in Zululand. A huge wedding was planned, with guests invited from far and wide. The lobolo was already promised, in return for a virginal wife. Chastity was a prized gift that belonged only to her husband, virginity fiercely guarded by the community, young girls were taught to take great pride in it. Women elders would be called upon to examine a young girl for this purpose and must verify her virginity. Any witness to the contrary could put her life in danger. In those days they were strict about purity. The parents of the betrothed had to guarantee it. Well, she was hardly virginal, and the shame of the baby...'

'So it wasn't the groom's child?'

'No. My guess is that it was someone else, not even from her own village.'

'So Martha was trying to hide the evidence.'

'She had suffered the secret alone. I knew she was hiding something.'

'What happened to Martha... and the girl, Rahab? Did she live?'

'She survived, yes. She might have ended in history's no-where-land, in the big city among migrant men. But the rest? I don't know.'

Joseph was right, a story ceases to be yours at a point of history when you exit and other people's lives carry on without you.

The rest was not my story.

III

This morning I sat and watched the leopard for the last time. No camera or sketch pad, just me in the purple shade and her in dappled gold sunlight.

I had set out early so that I could watch the sun rise over the Lubombos.

It was just light enough to make out the accustomed terrain of flat rockbeds, scrubs and aloes, and I picked my way down the plateau, a sure-footed and confident rockjumper. A family of dassies emerged warily from their hiding places and scrutinized this early morning intruder. They scattered away again, dark silhouettes slipping back into their semi-detached apartments.

The sky was turning a shade of blue I had no name for. Streaks of magenta clouds lay like abandoned evening shawls strewn across a dark satin sheet. I stood in my own silent space for a long time, awake to the splendour of this world and aware of the simple wonder of being.

As the sun topped the horizon, I made my way down towards the ironwood forest where she'd be waiting. She was lying there on the same branch, watching the cubs chasing imaginary prey amongst the leaves and twigs on the ground. I sat down a fair distance away, suddenly conscious that this time I was on my own. She looked up at me briefly and then looked away with a disinterest that could have been construed as mild disdain.

The leopard's attention was caught by one of the cubs that had moved away towards a tangle of shrubs and long grass. She half rose on her perch and turned herself towards him. The cub was preoccupied with a playful hunt of his own. I could not make out from that distance what he pounced upon. Whatever it was, he rolled over it, allowing it to limp away and began stalking it again. By the time he had arranged himself in position, wriggled his hindquarters and was poised to pounce, the reluctant plaything had moved on. It could have been a tiny tortoise or a grasshopper teasing the aspiring hunter to such comical antics.

But he was straying too far from the safety of his surrounds and the leopardess lifted herself wearily from the branch and leapt heavily down to the ground. She slowly padded over to her cub and examined the object of his fascination. A mother censuring his toys. She sniffed and poked it with her nose and lifted her head in a disinterested fashion. Then she slumped down and rolled over in the dust. She opened her mouth in a wide yawn, her teeth alarmingly vicious. Then she rolled over again and nudged the little one, but he was not to be distracted that easily. She dropped her paw across his back and bit his head so that he squealed and lay still. She held him there in her powerful jaws for a while until he submitted entirely. Then she let go and rose, moving back towards the base of the tree where the other cub was watching the outcome of this performance. The errant cub shook his head and stumbled clumsily after his mother. He had been suitably chastised.

The leopardess sat erect, surveying the horizon, her ears turning back to catch the morning sounds. I wanted to remember her this way, Queen of Felines, grand and sovereign.

I thought of Shaba.

I thought: She was the sum of what we all were.

For Thomas she was the elusive god of heroes, his passion once found and lost again. For the Dad she was the hunted, perhaps his own instinctive and untamed self, the evidence of which he sought to destroy, rather than own it and tame it within him. For my grandmother, the creature embodied her fears, of all things wild and primitive that might destroy her porcelain world. My mother, who spent a lifetime denying what was real, long refused to acknowledge that there was a leopard at all. For Martha she was Ingwe, the omen, Messenger of Great Troubles, the spirit of the beast that came to sit in her head and swallowed up her mind.

For me, the grown-up Gillian, she has become everything that speaks of this continent, an opportunist, a survivor, Mother of Africa, the she-predator and the prey of man. She is the embodiment of all that is beautiful and cruel in this Creation, but her intention has no premeditated malice. She simply is.

Is that what Thomas knew? She was the watcher and the watched, and in that anomalous situation, what was it that he saw and recognised?

Perhaps Hugh was the one who understood it best – Wild Beast or Feline Queen, the dichotomy of our gender – How shall men know thee?

In the privacy of my hotel room I plugged in my laptop and downloaded five weeks of mail messages. Hugh's e-mail was there, hidden amongst the mostly extraneous junk mail that littered the inbox.

From London with love.

It was a long letter, with apologies for the late reply: Just returned from Florence with Emily Trent (his mistress of twenty years or more) – 'loved Italy – wallowed in the works of art – ate decadent amounts of Italian food – indulged in bottles of wine daily and added kilos to an already extended waistline'.

Then the words I'd waited for, that I read and reread.

'We never spoke much about Thomas, or what happened when you left Swaziland. I wanted to, Jilly, but I wasn't sure if you were ready yet. We all have to face our shadows eventually, darling, and you are bravely facing this head-on. Alone. If only I could have been there to share the journey with you, but these old bones would never have survived weeks in the open bush anyway. When Thomas died my own grief was so unbearable, I removed myself from all of you. Selfishly. I can't imagine what it was like for you and Essie and my dear sister.

It has been so difficult to let go of the anger and the blame. I often wonder, if I had been there – if I could have done more… but after you all left for Rhodesia, it seemed impossible to intervene. Your lives were already mapped out. I still blame myself for allowing the nightmare to take its course.

But to settle the uncertain doubts you still have about the child, I will tell you what I know.

I returned to Swaziland in mid-February, a couple of weeks after you'd left. The horror of the story about the baby and the leopard was still fresh in the minds of the community. Amongst the black people it was already legendary. I spent an afternoon with a friend of mine who was a constable at the Mbabane police station. That was when I found out why Martha was never prosecuted, and why the leopard was a convenient scapegoat for the murder of the child. I gathered from your letter that you suspected something. The child was not black, Jilly. She was a coloured child, her eyes deep blue, a frizz of soft gold hair. Solomon had suspected a white father from the beginning. He finally told me the truth after much badgering. He was there that night at the compound when the girl Rahab was raped in Martha's room. He'd heard her scream. He saw the man running from her room that night, and found Rahab lying torn and terrified on the floor. They decided to keep her shame hidden, even from Martha. When the girl found herself pregnant she came back to her mother and was to stay in Swaziland until the child was born. Martha was sure at first that it was the child of the man she was to marry. At least they might have kept their disgrace a secret until after the marriage. It was only later, a week or two before the child was born, that Martha learnt the truth about its conception. She devised the plan to have the baby removed by the inyanga and buried on the hill, along with her daughter's disgrace. She was only trying to protect her virtue. The poor woman was caught in the middle of two restrictive social norms, two patriarchal societies that offered no room for escape.

By the time Shaba found the baby lying in the donga the baby had already been suffocated. The official medical examiner knew this. The leopardess carried her to the tree where she licked off all traces of the birth blood. She was clean and perfect when Solomon found her except for the two neat incisions and a broken neck. He had disturbed the leopard with his yelling. Thank God for that. One can only imagine…

Bryan was 'in' with the police captain. Perhaps he bribed him, perhaps he convinced him that the leopard was indeed the perpetrator. We'll never know. He honoured only one thing, and that was that Martha, Rahab and Solomon would not take the blame. Only because he was afraid of his own exposure, but the consequences of one act of entitlement were far reaching.

So, my lovely, that was the awful reality. In the broader sense, Bryan was the archetype of the bruised and bullied victim; his father was a cruel man, who became the controlling manipulator – an archetype still evident in the politics of Africa and so many other countries fraught with conflict and fraudulent democracies, black or white it makes no difference. He moves and acts under the opium of power, playing games with other people's lives. His perverse instinct obviates the greater good of mankind, in his blind acquiescence to his own fears and egocentric desires. He is the usurper of political power, the one who profits on the backs of broken nations, the husband and father who destroys the innocent trust of his family. This is where evil resides. To be fair, it resides in us all, in the shadowed landscape of our evolution, and coupled with human intention and self-serving individualism, it can assume dire consequences for us all.

For the leopard there can be no judgement.

Darling, don't mind the rambling of an old man who has only time left to pontificate the meaning of this madness we live in. I urge you to write this story, Jilly. It needs to be told.

I promise to see you in Africa at least one more time, when we can put all this behind us and indulge in a decadent week of music, food and wine – the only pleasures left for an old fool such as I.

Leave a pocket full of love in Swaziland from me.

Love you dearly.

Hugh

The child was not black. She was a coloured child.

It was the confirmation of what I somehow knew. Not from the beginning, but a slow dawning of realization.

There can be no half-half and step-step in our culture. It struck me, then, that out there above the blackened scrublands above the scorched and ravaged hill, lying face down in the branches of a thorn tree, that was Essie's sister. By some default, in the generous African way of ubuntu, she was also mine. A honey-coloured child was the mistake nobody wanted, long forgotten, discarded from the start, buried somewhere out there in Swazi soil.

A sister.

IV

I awoke after a sound sweet sleep that carried me into that deep and restful place beyond dreaming. I ate a huge breakfast off real china plates and drank cups of hot tea with real milk. There was only one more lap to my journey's end. I paid a fortune to the taxi driver who meandered around the suburb of clinker brick and stucco-walled houses to find the uncertain location of the old house. We drove around the hill along roads strange and unfamiliar. The houses up there were enveloped in shrubbery and abundant trees, behind high walls and prohibiting fences.

I stopped the car several times, disorientated. We tried a narrow rugged road to the right. It was the view of the mountains, and the valley below that stirred within me an uncanny recognition. The house stood on her own, somewhat removed from her neighbours, as if she had always preferred it that way. In her outward appearance she was too changed to stir much memory. But the stone chimneys, the front garden and the circular drive gave her away, the jacarandas now wide girthed and so tall.

A gracious Swazi woman dressed in a lilac linen suit came to the door. She nodded and smiled when I asked her if I could wander round the garden of my childhood. She answered me in the Queen's English; her manners were impeccably fine. The irony of this situation was hard to ignore. I smiled at the thought of our grandmother seeing this far into the future.

I walked round the house, its grandeur diminished through adult eyes. I stood at the top of the green kikuyu terrace. The pungent smell of freshly mown grass drifted keenly on the balmy summer air. The pines at the bottom of the lawn that were once saplings had grown into a forest of splendid fir trees.

The garden seemed smaller than I remembered it, the surrounding bush more tamed, less wild, encroached upon by other people's properties. Where PapaMac's vegetables grew in tended, manicured rows, a new house now stands, smart and defiant and oblivious.

I found the old grave, the sturdy column of river stones, shrouded in a grove of ferns and azalea shrubs neglected and forgotten. I stroked the clouded brass plaque embedded in the cement.

Here lies Rufus, a trusted friend forever.

I allowed the tears then.

I cried for love, and the loss of Martha, my African mother who always listened, who cherished us and laughed with us, and for the madness that came that night and never left. And for my grandmother who saw things before they happened, from a secret place of knowing. She died exactly four years after the black birds finally found an open window and flew away with PapaMac's uncertain heart. Our Gaga hoped to keep the naked savages out of her treasured world. Afraid of the harsh nature of a continent she didn't understand.

I cried for our sister buried in the red Swazi soil.

And Thomas. My brother never came back here after all.

Two children once lived here, laughed here in a garden of innocent pleasures and ran circles round a dog's grave, building a stone mound of hidden bones and rusted metal things on a black and burnt hill so they'd never forget that time, that Place of Heaven.

EPILOGUE

We left Swaziland in 1960. It was a year of turmoil in southern Africa, political unease that wrote the beginnings of a new history. For thirty years the struggle continued.

It was to take another seven years before Swaziland became a sovereign state. There were many like us who left, who kept leaving, afraid, running from a history that might eventually overtake them and swallow their white skin. Some stayed, however, and their children grew into the soil of the land, weathering the change and hoping to make a difference.

We left Swaziland to begin our new life in Rhodesia. The Dad, like so many who could not envisage a life beyond the fantasy of unlimited supremacy, was trying to hold onto the last bastions of colonialism. Rhodesia was as yet not too troubled by militant and angry hoards of tribal natives, and white society was still thriving comfortably in a quasi-British lifestyle.

Thomas and I rode to our new school on new bicycles. We lived in a spacious double-storey house on a wide street lined with tall gum trees. Our mother planted a pretty garden with lawn and shrubs and flowers with the names of English girls. There was a dog and a cat, and a television set. The sound of clinking glass and ice tinkled from porches in the evenings as grown-ups settled in cane veranda chairs and enjoyed cigarettes and sundowners before a late dinner, while the children played cricket or simply ran around the wide lawns in their pyjamas. We had a house boy called Ephraim and a belligerent maid who treated other people's laundry and children with equal indifference. We were a normal family with the usual domestic obligations and frustrations, but at least we never needed to live with other people again.

My mother once told me that if Hell did exist it would be filled with pleas for extenuating circumstances. Most people who end up bad are simply acting out a performance written in the script of an uncertain childhood, she said. My mother was more tolerant than most. Even the lost boys couldn't wear down her unlimited patience.

The Dad eventually became the man that I had somehow recognised glimpses of over the years, as only a child can sometimes see into the true heart of an adult.

Drunk fathers do stupid things, Lally said once. You just do what you're told and don't tell, she told me when I was seven. We were the same after all, daughters of fathers who wanted us grown up before our time and no one to tell because you didn't talk about things like that. Lally, who grew tall and extremely beautiful, became a top model in Jo'burg in the mid-sixties, was married to an alcoholic from Durban for a while, and ended up with a sugar cane farmer from Empangeni where she lost her figure to four children and a mountain of sweetness.

Thomas? He had grown so far from his heart that he preferred no one's company but his own. I couldn't talk to him any more. In never letting the Dad win, he lost his outward vulnerability; there was a hard determination in him I couldn't understand. I thought at times that infatuation had won him over, but he met too many of the Dad's challenges in grim and calculated contest. Thomas died too young, playing war games for a country he never believed in. But he had left us all a long time before.

My story is complete.

I am Gillian grown up a little more, still floating precariously between two continents, belonging somewhere in between. I no longer dream of leopards.

But watching her on the plains of the Lubombos has begun a restoration, like the slow and deliberate washing away of layers of grime from an old painting. I suppose Nature does that to the keen observer, an open window to wider possibilities, the perfect balance, the ebb and flow, the beginning and end. She expects nothing in return. This Africa, this place of our heaven is harsh, but not without forgiveness.

I think I have glimpsed a sense of the God that Thomas once came to know in her. His leopard. I was to find my brother's final answer to me in one particular moment of wakefulness. It was in my last encounter with the leopard.

The sky had turned a gentle blue, the clouds had separated into lazy white wisps slowly diminishing under the bold scrutiny of the sun. It was going to be one of those hot dusty days.

A sudden move to retrieve my rucksack from the dust startled her, and she lifted her head, her shoulder muscles taut with apprehension. She rose up slowly onto all fours and started moving towards me, slowly, ambling forward, half curious I imagine, but her flattened ears indicated a defensive stance.

I was unprepared. She walked steadily forward, her marble eyes holding me stone still. Then she stopped suddenly and sat down, not more than twelve metres between us.

I am at your mercy here, I thought.

There is no moral distinction. Hers is not a choice, not a measuring of consequence. Instinct. Not only for her sole survival, but for her kind. Nature is played out in her every move. No blame here. I lowered my eyes in humble submission.

I'm not sure how long we remained there facing each other, but I felt myself letting go of thought, of fear, until all that was left was the clear clean awareness of being, of knowing. In that eternal moment we were the same. In truth I had come face to face with my self.

When I glanced up again she was walking away from me, and back to the cubs. She heaved herself up into the branches and returned to her perch in the tree.

I stayed a while and watched as the light cast patches of gold on her back. Then I turned my back on her and walked away, up the rocky slope towards the camp.